D1365101

The Matchmaking
Machine

 This Large Print Book carries the
Seal of Approval of N.A.V.H.

The Matchmaking Machine

Judith McWilliams

Thorndike Press • Waterville, Maine

Published in 2006 by arrangement with Harlequin Books S.A.

Thorndike Press® Large Print Romance.

The tree indicium is a trademark of Thorndike Press.

The text of this Large Print edition is unabridged.
Other aspects of the book may vary from the original edition.

Set in 16 pt. Plantin.

Printed in the United States on permanent paper.

Library of Congress Cataloging-in-Publication Data

McWilliams, Judith.
    The matchmaking machine / by Judith McWilliams.
      p. cm. — (Thorndike Press large print romance)
    ISBN 0-7862-8892-2 (lg. print : hc : alk. paper)
    1. Women computer programmers — Fiction.
  2. Revenge — Fiction. 3. Large type books. I. Title.
  II. Series: Thorndike Press large print romance series.
  PS3563.C95M37 2006
  813'.54—dc22   2006014521

The Matchmaking
Machine

Chapter One

She was going to teach John Worthington a long-overdue lesson in humility if it was the last thing she ever did, Maggie Romer told herself as she nervously tightened her grip on the thick manila envelope she was carrying. Taking a deep breath, she punched in the security code she'd been given to get into Worthington's apartment building. The oversized glass doors obediently slid open.

Maggie stepped into the spacious lobby and looked around, trying to ignore her feeling of inferiority in the face of such opulent luxury. She was no longer an unwanted foster kid on the outside looking in, she reminded herself. These days, she was a well-paid, highly trained computer professional.

She was also a woman on a mission. Her soft pink lips tightened as an image of Sam Moore's haggard features popped into her mind. According to his wife, he was so depressed that he just sat around all day, staring at the wall.

Sam might be powerless, but *she* wasn't, and she was determined to get revenge for him. No, not revenge. Justice.

Justice was everyone's right. Worthington might be the company's new owner, but that didn't give him the right to summarily fire Sam and then refuse to give him a reference. What Worthington had done was unconscionable. Sam was great at what he did. Not only that, but he was super to work for. She didn't know a single person in the entire company who had a bad word to say about him — man or woman. Yet Worthington had dismissed him without even so much as a reference. And without a reference and an explanation for the firing, potential employers would assume that Sam was incompetent and had only held his job as president because he was the old owner's son-in-law. The entire office was in agreement that Worthington deserved to be called to account for his actions.

In fact, Emily, Sam's former secretary, hated John Worthington so much she hadn't even been willing to deliver an important report to his empty apartment, despite the fact that he wasn't due to arrive from California until later tonight.

When Maggie had heard Emily vilifying

Worthington in the lunchroom, she immediately volunteered to drop the document off for her. As far as Maggie was concerned, getting access to his apartment was a heaven-sent opportunity to check the place out for clues about his personal likes and dislikes.

Trying to act as if she belonged in this kind of setting, Maggie walked across the lobby toward the sour-faced guard sitting behind a desk near the elevators. He straightened slightly as she approached, and the furtive gleam of sexual desire that lightened his eyes sent a chill of revulsion down her spine. She bit the inside of her lip as she fought her instinctive urge to hunch her shoulders in an attempt to hide her breasts.

"I'm Maggie Romer delivering a package for John Worthington. Emily Adams from Computer Solutions should have already called to tell you I'd be coming," she told the guard.

"She did. And I told her that I was the only one on and couldn't leave the desk to go up with you. She said you didn't need an escort." He shrugged. "That's fine by me, but tell her I said if there's a problem not to come to me about it."

Maggie nodded and walked into one of

the open elevators. Taking out the plastic card Emily had given her that provided access to the penthouse level, Maggie inserted it into the slot in the control panel.

Nothing will go wrong, she told herself, trying to ignore the feeling of impending doom that engulfed her as the elevator doors snapped shut. She'd leave the envelope on his desk in the study as Emily had instructed and then take a quick look around for any information about his personal habits that she could enter into the program she had written about John Worthington.

A sense of satisfaction filled her at the thought of the novel computer application she had come up with in her quest to teach Worthington a lesson. She'd been listening to a couple of her friends talk about their experiences with Internet dating when she suddenly realized that it should be possible to create a program that would tell her exactly what kind of woman John Worthington found attractive. After all, those Internet dating sites found potentially compatible mates all the time. And if she could do that, there was the possibility — even if it was a slim one — that she could turn herself into something close to his idea of perfection and get him to fall for her. Then, once he'd committed himself, she could laugh in his face and walk out, letting him find out what it felt like to be rejected. To be treated as if *he* were a thing of absolutely no value. Job, be darned.

Even though Maggie had created the program, she knew her plan was a long shot. Still, there were several points in her favor.

For one, Worthington's electronics empire was headquartered in San Francisco, and, now that his father was semiretired, he spent most of his time there with occasional trips to the company's offices in the far east. His presence in New York was so rare that there had been speculation in the financial press that his allocation of six whole weeks to oversee the integration of their software company into the parent company meant that Worthington was positioning himself to move into the applications side of computers.

Maggie reasoned that since Worthington was a stranger in town, he wouldn't know anyone, and since he wasn't planning on staying, he probably wouldn't bother with the local social scene. That would drastically limit the number of women competing with her for his attention.

Second, as a key member of his staff, she

11

would see him at the office on a regular basis. The opportunity was definitely there if she could take advantage of it. She'd considered the possibility that he might not be willing to date an employee, but she quickly pushed that aside. Interoffice dating was more common than companies liked to admit, and when he saw that she was the woman of his dreams, how could be resist?

Once her program had spelled out what his ideal woman looked like, Maggie had completely revamped her image to conform to it as closely as possible. Her plain brown hair now sported reddish highlights and fell to her shoulders in a sexy tumble of loose curls, and her pleasing, if unspectacular, features were enhanced by the best makeup money could buy. As for her clothes . . .

She winced slightly as she caught sight of herself in the mirrors that lined three of the four elevator walls. She'd started wearing her new wardrobe two weeks ago so that all the surprised comments from colleagues about her wearing something other than her usual nondescript suits and comfortable sweaters would be over before Worthington arrived in town.

Unfortunately, she'd discovered that two

weeks wasn't long enough for her to feel comfortable with her new image. She shifted uncomfortably as she studied the way her black slacks clung to her slender hips before faithfully outlining her long, slim legs. A lifetime might not be enough, she conceded.

The elevator came to a smooth stop on the top floor and the doors opened onto a discreetly lighted foyer carpeted in a soft dove-gray. There was a real floral arrangement sitting on a gilt table beside the door to the penthouse apartment.

Maggie straightened her shoulders, trying to ignore the way her action tightened her black silk shirt over her small, high breasts. She was determined to teach Worthington a lesson, and if dressing sexier was what it took, then that's what she'd do.

With anticipation, Maggie took out the key to Worthington's apartment Emily had given her. Unlocking the door, she slipped inside.

A soundless whistle escaped her as she took in the wall of glass in the living room that gave her a panoramic view of Central Park twenty stories below. Money might not buy happiness, but it sure could buy beautiful surroundings, she thought. The room looked like something out of a decorating book for the seriously rich.

John Worthington certainly believed in pampering himself, although . . .

Maggie frowned slightly as she took in the chintz prints on the sofas and over-stuffed chairs. From the extensive research she'd already done on him, she would have guessed that his taste in furniture leaned more toward priceless antiques. This room seemed out of character with the image of him on her program. Maybe the taste reflected here wasn't Worthington's.

She knew from what Emily had said that Worthington hated living in hotels and one of the first things his advanceman, Daniel Romanos, had done when he'd arrived in town last week had been to lease his boss this apartment. Maybe Romanos had leased it furnished?

Hmm . . . What now? Did she enter a liking for chintz and English country into her program or put in that Worthington was adaptable enough to live with decor not to his taste? She didn't know which was more accurate, but of one thing she was certain: the program was becoming a lot more complicated than she'd originally anticipated. The variables seemed both endless and endlessly fascinating.

Maggie walked farther into the room, wondering if any of Worthington's personal effects had arrived yet. According to Emily, his flight wasn't due to arrive until after midnight, but he could have shipped some of his stuff along with Daniel Romanos.

She reached down to open the drawer in the end table beside one of the sofas when she heard a loud clanging sound coming from down the hallway to her left. A shiver ran down her spine and she automatically took a step back toward the front door before common sense told her that it couldn't be a burglar. For one thing, it was too hard to get into the building. For another, one of the first requirements of burglarizing would be quietness. And whomever it was had made no attempt to be quiet.

Maybe Worthington had sent his housekeeper from San Francisco ahead to get the place ready for him, she thought in a sudden burst of excitement. A housekeeper who might be able to give her personal facts about him firsthand. So far, all her information about Worthington had been gleaned secondhand from magazine and newspaper articles.

Eagerly, Maggie headed toward the

sound. At the very least, she could ask whomever it was where the study was so she could drop off the envelope and do some snooping in his desk drawers.

Maggie quickly located where the noise was coming from. Sticking her head around the half-open door, she peered inside. Her eyes widened when she saw the bottom half of a man sticking out from beneath the bathroom vanity. Her mouth dried and she slowly ran the tip of her tongue over her lower lip as her eyes measured the impressive breadth of his chest before wandering down over his flat stomach to linger on the long, lean length of his denim-clad thighs.

I wonder what the rest of him looks like? she thought, suppressing an urge to look under the cabinet and find out. Why had she never found a plumber built like that? Her apartment building was serviced by a surly, middle-aged man with a beer belly who wouldn't raise a lustful thought in a nymphomaniac, while this guy . . .

She took a deep, steadying breath as her gaze returned of its own volition to his tight jeans.

"Excuse me," she began then instinctively jerked back when the man's body suddenly jackknifed. There was a hollow ringing sound as what she assumed was his head hit something hard under the cabinet.

Maggie barely registered the curse that rolled out from beneath the cabinet. She was far more interested in the deep, dark, velvety tone of his voice. It lapped enticingly against her skin, nudging each and every nerve ending she owned to eager, expectant life. Her breath caught in her lungs in anticipation as the man wiggled out from under the cabinet. A powerful surge of awareness engulfed her as she got her first clear look at him.

The top half of him was even better than the bottom half, she realized in astonishment. His ink-black hair was cut slightly shorter than the present style and disheveled, as if he'd been running his fingers through it. She would have expected an olive complexion with hair that dark, but his skin was a pale honey-gold that gave his gray eyes an almost crystalline look. Her gaze slipped down over the thin blade of his nose to land on his wide mouth and all rational thought was suspended as she was instantly consumed by a desire to press her lips to his.

"Are you deaf, as well?" the man bit out.

Maggie opened her mouth to ask as well

as what and then thought better of the idea. She didn't want to start the conversation by trading insults, and she was pretty sure there was one buried in his question.

Ignoring his comment would probably be the quickest way to lower the sudden tension which had sprung up between them, she decided.

"Did you hurt your head?" she tried.

"Yes," he snapped. "I probably fractured my skull."

"Nonsense," Maggie said bracingly. "All you did was smack it on something."

"That something was a porcelain sink!" He gave her an aggrieved look that made her want to take him in her arms and kiss his ill humor away, something she didn't recall ever wanting to do with anyone before.

"Sit down." Maggie gestured toward the vanity seat. "I'll see how bad it is."

To her surprise, he obediently sat down and bent his head slightly so she could look.

Maggie set the manila envelope and her purse down on the vanity and tentatively touched his head. Her fingers sank into his silky, dark hair, searching for a lump. His hair was cool on the outside and very warm next to his scalp. It was an intriguing combination. From this close, she could smell the citrusy scent of his cologne.

Maggie swallowed uneasily as a curl of heat tightened in the pit of her stomach, making her feel edgy. Her fingertips began to tingle, and she had to fight the urge to caress the very slight bump she found.

"I think you'll live." Her voice came out sounding husky and not at all like her normal, even, no-nonsense tone. How could she be reacting so strongly to some strange man she had chanced upon in a bathroom? She wondered uneasily. She had never been the impulsive type about anything — and that included sexual attraction. Not only that, but she didn't know the first thing about this guy.

No, that wasn't quite true, she corrected herself. She actually knew two things about him. She knew he was gorgeous, and she knew he was a plumber.

He might live, but he wouldn't do it with any degree of comfort in her vicinity, Richard Worthington thought ruefully as he struggled to control his body's enthusiastic response to her touch. He certainly didn't want her to realize that he'd taken one look at her and every male hormone he had had kicked into overdrive — at least, not until he figured out who she was and what she was doing in his apartment.

He was positive he'd locked the door behind him, so she had to have had a key to have gotten in. Could she have come from the office of the lawyer who was handling his sublease of the place? One thing was clear: she certainly hadn't come to steal anything because she had no place to hide it. His gaze lingered on the small expanse of delectable-looking skin between her formfitting sweater and her pants. The blackness of her outfit highlighted the creamy texture of her perfect skin.

"I'm Richard, and you are . . ." He held out his hand, seizing the opportunity to touch her.

The woman put her hand in his.

"Maggie. Do you know where the housekeeper is?" she said, looking uncomfortable, as if she wasn't used to dealing with unknown men.

"What housekeeper?" Richard looked around the spacious bathroom as if he expected to find a strange woman hiding in a corner. "There was no one else here when I arrived earlier."

"Oh," Maggie said and glanced down, only to find that she was still holding on to his hand like a lifeline. Appearing to be embarrassed, she dropped it and took a step back. "Tell me, have you seen the study?"

"Why?" he said curiously.

"I'm supposed to put that on the desk in the study." She nodded toward the manila envelope on the vanity.

"What's in it?" Richard leaned over and began to search through the toolbox on the floor.

"I don't know," she said. "I'm just the messenger."

"Here, hold this." Richard handed her the wrench and went back to rummaging through his tools.

Maggie automatically accepted it, though she seemed to be rather surprised by its weight.

"Open the envelope and see what it is," Richard ordered, wondering if it was the treasurer's report that was supposed to have arrived earlier. Straightening out the mess Sam had created was not going to be an easy job — he felt a surge of adrenaline at the thought of the challenge — but it would be worth it. Both he and his father agreed that the company was the perfect vehicle to use to get a foothold in the software applications market.

"Certainly not!" Maggie snapped. "And why are you so interested? Unless you're an industrial spy?"

With narrowed eyes, she studied his arrested expression. His gray eyes were blank, and his mouth had fallen slightly open, revealing perfect white teeth. Could he actually be such a thing? She wondered uncertainly. On the surface, it seemed like a ludicrous idea because, until Worthington actually arrived, there should have been nothing of any business import in the apartment for him to spy on. He could hardly have known that someone would be coming by with an envelope from the treasurer, could he? She wasn't sure. The only thing she knew about industrial spying had been learned at the movies, which was hardly a reliable source of information.

"Are you serious?" Richard asked, studying her suspicious face, unable to decide whether to be amused or annoyed. Clearly she had no idea that he owned the company that had hired her messenger firm to deliver the package. Who did she think he was? Her next words answered his question.

"No, not really, but I think you'd better stick to the plumbing you were hired to do."

Could she really think he was a plumber? He wondered in confusion. Or was this some clever ploy to . . . To do what? No

22

one knew he was in New York yet except Daniel, and he wouldn't willingly give anyone the time of day, let alone information about him.

"You're very loyal to your boss," he probed as he inched back under the sink.

"No, I'm not," she said, allowing herself the self-indulgent pleasure of openly eyeing his body while he couldn't see her. "What I do have is a strongly developed sense of survival. I don't even want to think about what he'd do if he found out I'd looked at his precious papers!"

"I suppose anyone who operated a messenger service would have to be extra careful about her company's reputation," he said. "Hand me the wrench I asked you to hold." Richard stuck a large hand out from under the sink.

Maggie gave it to him. "I don't work for a messenger service. I work for a computer firm that was just bought out by a big electronics holding company from California. The son of the owner is coming to town to oversee the takeover, and, from what I've seen, he makes Simon Legree look like an advocate for human rights. The person who should have delivered this package was the old president's secretary, and she flatly refused to even come near this place. That's how bad Worthington is."

Richard's hand stilled as her words sank in. She was referring to him, he realized in shock. But why did she dislike him so much? Unless office gossip was responsible? Rumors did tend to be rife during a takeover.

"What exactly are you doing?" Maggie threw into the silence. She'd much rather talk about Worthington than her problems at work.

"I'm replacing the cold-water pipe to the faucet," he said, deciding not to tell her who he was just yet.

"I need a Phillips screwdriver. Do you know what one looks like?"

"Of course I know what a Phillips head screwdriver looks like. The days of the helpless little woman are long gone."

"Oh, I don't know. There's something kind of appealing about knowing more than a woman about guy things."

"There are no *guy* things. That's . . ." Her voice trailed away as her eyes instinctively dropped to his groin and the muscles in her abdomen suddenly clenched. Okay, so there were some *exclusively* guy things, but she had no intention of amending her original statement and opening up what could prove to be an embarrassing line of discussion.

24

"Okay, traditional guy things, then," Richard said. "Turn on the faucet, will you?"

Maggie obediently turned on the faucet and yelped when cold water spurted up, soaking the front of her sweater. Hastily, she jumped back. To her dismay, the heel of her shoe caught on the edge of his body and she tripped, landing on him.

The feel of his hard body beneath her soft hips had a curiously enervating effect on her. All she wanted to do was stay there and absorb the feel of his flesh pressing into hers. He felt so good. So . . .

"Are you all right?" Richard demanded, as Maggie winced. The man must think she was a total klutz.

Hurriedly, she scrambled off him and muttered, "Other than being drenched, I'm fine."

"Sorry about that, but getting wet is one of the hazards of being a plumber's helper," Richard said in a cool tone that was totally at odds with the interest in his eyes as he moved from under the sink and noted the way her wet sweater was plastered to her breasts.

"I am not a plumber's helper. I'm simply an innocent bystander. A wet innocent bystander."

"I should be able to do something about the wet part. I replaced a washer in the sink in the kitchen earlier and there's a washer and dryer in there. We'll just throw your sweater and bra in the dryer. Since no one's living here yet, no one will mind."

Maggie felt her cheeks heat at his casual reference to her underwear. It appeared that even the plumber was more sophisticated than she was.

She shook her head, sending the damp ends of her curls flying. "It's too risky. Suppose Worthington decided to catch an earlier flight. I can just imagine his reaction if he walked in and found me wrapped in a towel. Besides, I don't make it a habit to take off my clothes in front of strange men." *Even handsome ones,* she silently added.

Actually, she was pretty sure she knew exactly what Worthington's reaction would be, she thought grimly. One of the strongest dislikes her program had registered was that he hated being chased — apparently even more than he hated publicity. Which probably accounted for the fact that the only photograph she had been able to find of him had been a grainy long-distance shot that looked like it had been taken through a heavy fog. Even the holding company's website hadn't included a single photo of her quarry, only of his father, the titular head of the company, John Worthington, Sr.

"We'll hear him if he shows up, and I'll distract him with a report on his plumbing while you retrieve your clothes. In the meantime, you can wear my shirt."

Richard casually stripped it off and handed it to her.

"The guard downstairs told me to make a pot of coffee if I wanted to," he lied. "Why don't you change while I fix us some? I'm ready for a break anyway."

Normally, Maggie would have never considered the offer, but she was due back at the office and showing up in soaking wet clothes just wouldn't do. Unfortunately, she didn't have enough time to run back to her own apartment to change. Spending the next fifteen to twenty minutes letting her stuff dry was her best option.

Cautiously, she reached for his shirt, her entire attention focused on his bare chest. It was covered by a thick wedge of curly black hair that arrowed downward, disappearing into the waistband of his jeans.

Maggie's breathing shortened as in her imagination her fingers followed that line of silky hair down his body, all the way down his body. She shivered as goose-bumps popped up on her arms.

"You're chilled." Richard misinterpreted her reaction.

"Hurry up and get out of those wet clothes."

Stepping around her, he left, quietly closing the door behind him.

Maggie released her breath on a long, wistful sigh, then blinked when she could still see the enticing vision of his bare chest in her mind's eye.

"Okay, so you've got a bad case of the hots for the plumber," she muttered to herself. "There's nothing wrong with that. You're a normal woman. Why shouldn't you respond to male perfection when you find it?"

Heat twisted through her abdomen at the thought of just *how* enthusiastically she'd like to respond.

Chance was a fine thing, she thought ruefully as she pulled her sweater over her head. She might lust after him, but she'd seen no sign that he felt anything at all when he looked at her.

What kind of woman would appeal to Richard? She wondered and immediately thought of her program. Unfortunately, there was no way she could apply it to a normal man. It was only high-profile ones like John Worthington that she could find out enough information about to use it on.

She frowned as she remembered why she was here in the first place. Unfortunately, her plan to check the apartment for clues to Worthington's personality wasn't going to get very far with Richard here. He might be taking full advantage of his boss's offer to use the facilities, but she doubted that he'd stand by and let her snoop in drawers. He'd be afraid that she might take something and he'd get blamed.

The vexing problem of getting even with John Worthington slipped from her mind as she pulled Richard's softly worn denim shirt on and the citrusy scent of his cologne drifted into her lungs, speeding up her heart rate and making her nerves tighten. Trying to ignore the unsettling sensation, Maggie buttoned the shirt and then rolled up the sleeves so that she could use her hands. Picking up her wet clothes, the manila envelope and her purse, she went to look for the kitchen.

She had no trouble finding it. She simply followed the tantalizing smell of freshly brewed coffee. She walked into the large room decorated entirely in white — white tile floor, white walls, white cabinets and white ceiling. Even the appliances were white.

"This place could double as an operating room," she said as she handed Richard her wet clothes. "Make sure you use the delicate low-heat option."

He opened a pair of white louvered doors on the opposite wall to reveal a tiny laundry room. He tossed her damp things into the white dryer, set it and turned it on.

"I think the owner is into the utilitarian look. Either that or he never comes into the kitchen, so he doesn't care how stark it looks. Help yourself to some coffee." Richard gestured toward the steaming pot.

Maggie set her envelope and purse down on the counter, took one of the mugs hanging from a cast-iron holder and poured herself a cup. She sat down on a bar stool at the Corian breakfast bar.

"I hope they don't take long to dry. I want to get out of here before Worthington shows. Did whoever hired you tell you when he was scheduled to arrive?" she asked.

Maggie noticed his slight frown and assumed it was because he didn't know whom she was talking about. "Or weren't you told whom you were doing the job for?"

Thoughtfully, Richard took a drink of his coffee as he tried to decide what to do. He didn't like lying, even by omission, but the idea of telling Maggie the truth appealed to him even less. If he did, she would probably walk out, and he didn't want her to. He wanted the chance to get to know her better. Much better.

He'd been intrigued by her from the moment he'd first he'd seen her. Her gleaming brown hair with its reddish highlights and her deep blue eyes appealed to his aesthetic sense, while the perfection of her slender, long legs made him fantasize about what it would feel like to have them wrapped around him.

Richard studied her over the rim of her coffee cup. She really did think he was the plumber, which meant that the sexual interest he could see in her eyes every time she looked at him was for him and not his money. The knowledge sent a fizz of anticipation zinging through his bloodstream — an anticipation vaguely tinged with worry as he remembered her very unflattering opinion of him. Would that spark of interest die when she found out who he really was? And she would have to find out. There was no way he could keep his identity a secret from her indefinitely. Once he showed up at the office on Monday, everyone would be jostling for a glimpse of him. But that was Monday, and this was only Friday. He had a little time before he had to tell her the truth — time enough to convince her that the nasty rumors circulating in the office about him obviously had no basis in fact.

He frowned as Maggie's eyes suddenly widened in shock.

"Ugh!" she gasped and set the mug down with a thump. "What is this?" She stared into the stygian depths of the cup with disbelief.

"Just coffee," Richard said. "I made it myself."

"I certainly wouldn't advertise the fact," she shot back. "You might be held responsible for the results. This stuff could double as paint remover."

"I can't stand it weak."

"And I can't stand getting my week's allotment of caffeine in one shot." Maggie got up and poured half the brew down the sink. Then she added water, a large spoonful of sugar and a hefty dose of milk.

"Milk and sugar ruin the flavor of good coffee," he said.

"This is *not* good coffee," Maggie said, cautiously taking a sip of the resulting mixture. "Strong, yes. Good, no. And don't tell me it's a guy thing. Bad is bad."

"Ha, you probably make instant. Your taste buds need educating."

"If I drank much of this stuff, my taste buds would be more likely to be dissolved than educated. It . . ."

She tensed as she heard the chimes from the front door.

Was that Worthington? She wondered in dismay as Richard got up to answer it. But Worthington wouldn't knock on his own apartment door, would he? Surely, he'd have a key.

She didn't know, but she had no intention of guessing — and guessing wrong. She didn't want to meet him yet. She wanted their first meeting to take place on ground of her choosing, not his. Hurriedly, she grabbed the envelope and rushed after Richard, catching up with him at the front door.

"Don't open that," she whispered to Richard.

He paused, his hand halfway to the doorknob. "Why not?"

"I don't want to meet anyone wearing your shirt."

"How about if I just call through the door and tell them to come back when the dryer goes off."

"Don't be silly," she muttered.

"Me?!"

"I need to put this envelope on the desk the way I was told to. Stall whomever is out there while I find the study."

The person rang the bell again.

"Wait a minute. We're stalling," Richard yelled through the door.

"Honestly!" Maggie gave him an exasperated look. "This is important. That could be Worthington."

"It can't be Worthington," Richard said. "The guard at the front desk was specific about him not arriving until after I was finished."

"Then if you know so much, who is it?"

"Who are you?" Richard yelled through the door.

"Daniel Romanos," the voice called back.

"Damn!" Maggie scowled. "It's almost as bad. That's Worthington's hatchet man. Stall him."

She raced down the hall and pulled open an oak door. To her relief, it was the study. She pitched the manila envelope onto the middle of the bare desk and hurried back to the living room and Richard.

"Is the evidence hidden?" Richard asked.

"I wasn't *hiding* it. I was just putting it

where it belongs." Where she should have put it the minute she arrived — and would have if she hadn't been distracted by him.

Her eyes lingered on the firm line of his dark jaw. And it had been fatally easy to get sidetracked, too, she conceded honestly. There was something about Richard that made everything else fade into the background. It was a reaction she'd never had before, and it worried her. This was not the time for her to finally discover a man who appealed to her sexually — not when she had everything in place to launch her plan of revenge against Worthington.

Chapter Two

"So tell me, Sherlock, what am I supposed to do about our visitor?" Richard asked.

"Why ask me?"

"Because you're the one who told me not to open the door."

"I didn't mean permanently," she said and then hastily lowered her voice, having no idea just how solid the door was. She most emphatically didn't want Romanos to know she was here. He couldn't report what he didn't know to Worthington.

"Maybe if we just ignore him, he'll go away?" she suggested hopefully.

Richard frowned as Daniel suddenly got more insistent and began to pound on the door. Normally, he appreciated his personal assistant's dogged determination to get things done, but in this instance, it threatened to mess up his plans for Maggie.

"Impatient soul, isn't he?" Maggie said. "You sure can tell he's Worthington's right-hand man."

Richard ignored the pounding. Daniel

could wait. For what he paid the man, he could wait quietly, too.

"Why do you say that?" Richard asked curiously.

"Because according to office gossip, Worthington is a real mover and shaker in the business world. That type never waits patiently, so it makes sense that he would surround himself with the same kind of people. And with Worthington due to arrive in New York tonight, it also makes sense that his assistant would want to report in as soon as possible. I'm just surprised he isn't camped out at the airport."

Impeccable logic, Richard thought. As smart as she was, it would be impossible to fool her for any length of time, but he hoped keeping his identity a secret from Maggie would be possible for at least one night.

Maggie winced as Daniel attacked the door again.

"He clearly has no intention of going peacefully into the night," she said regretfully. "We're going to have to let him in."

"I could try telling him to go away and come back later," Richard suggested. Whether Daniel would or not depended on whether or not he recognized Richard's voice through the distorting effects of the wood.

"I think we've tried his patience enough," she said with a glum look at the entrance. She could almost feel the hostility bristling through it.

"Why don't you go see if your sweater and bra are dry while I let the guy in. I'll give him my best ain't-nobody-here-but-the-plumber routine."

Only too happy not to have to face Daniel, whom she'd met Monday when he'd arrived from San Francisco and disliked at first sight, Maggie hurried back into the kitchen. This had been the most unsettling day. And meeting Richard had been the defining point. Who would have thought that she would find the most appealing man she'd ever met under a cabinet in a strange bathroom.

Not that she'd met that many men, she conceded. Mostly, she just avoided them. It was safer that way. Men were a huge complication that she hadn't been able to afford in her life. She had been too busy, first studying and then working to establish her career. Too busy proving to herself that she wasn't the least bit like her mother. Or her father. The acid burn of anger that thoughts of her father always engendered overwhelmed her and she briefly closed her eyes, took a deep breath and resolutely banished him back to oblivion, where he belonged.

Stepping into the minuscule laundry room, she pulled the louvered doors closed behind her before yanking open the dryer door and pulling out her sweater and bra. They were still damp, but she put them on anyway in case she needed to make a quick escape. If Daniel was here, Worthington wouldn't be far behind. And she didn't want to meet Worthington now. She intended to orchestrate their first encounter very carefully. She would project the image of a bright, confident, sophisticated woman. The only kind of woman likely to attract his interest, according to her program. At the moment, she felt — and undoubtedly looked — like a frazzled refugee from a hectic day at the office.

Richard opened the front door, catching Daniel with his fist raised to pound on the door again.

"Be quiet," Richard ordered with a quick look over his shoulder to make sure Maggie was still in the kitchen. "Pretend you don't know me."

"Hell, Richard, in this mood, I'm not sure I *do* know you."

Richard grinned. "I'm doing some undercover work. The report from the treasurer's office is in the study, second door on the right." He gestured toward the room Maggie had entered. "Make a copy of it and send it by courier to Baxter at the San Francisco office. Don't fax anything," Richard said.

"Will do. Oh, and Wilton called. He said he'd located a man named Zylinski in Washington, D.C., who's a wizard at tracing embezzled funds through computers. I have a call in to him. I hope to hear from him tonight, or tomorrow morning, at the latest."

"Promise him anything, but get him here immediately to trace the movement of the money Moore embezzled. Wright's widow might have been willing to eat the losses to avoid sending her son-in-law to jail, but I want to know if Moore had any accomplices that are still with the company. Two million dollars in just three years is a hell of a lot of money for one person to lose playing poker even if he is a compulsive gambler."

Daniel shook his head. "It's a damn shame. Moore was one helluva salesman. He practically revitalized that company single-handedly after Wright had his first heart attack."

"Yeah, and then he bled it dry. I still

think Mrs. Wright was wrong. Son-in-law or not, she should have pressed charges against Moore."

Daniel looked into Richard's hard gray eyes and shivered. He sure wouldn't want to cross Richard. He was not a forgiving man.

"Lock the door behind you and let me know as soon as you hear from the computer expert," Richard said.

"Will do." Daniel hurried down the hallway to the study while Richard went back into the kitchen. A sound from behind the closed laundry-room doors told him where Maggie was.

"I got rid of him," Richard addressed the doors. "It's safe to come out."

Maggie opened the door and emerged, giving him a repressive look. "I wasn't hiding," she lied. "I was changing my clothes. Here's your shirt, and thank you."

She watched regretfully as he slipped into it and his magnificent, hairy chest disappeared from view.

"You can express your thanks by helping me connect the faucet back up again."

"If you'll remember correctly, that's how I got wet in the first place," she pointed out as she followed him back to the bathroom. Somehow, she seemed unable to resist the temptation of being around him. Maybe her makeover had changed more than just her outward appearance, she considered. Maybe wearing an up-to-the-minute hairstyle and sexy clothes had changed her outlook. Maybe *dressing* sexy made a woman more likely to *act* sexy. Kind of a variation on form following function? It was an unsettling thought.

"That was an accident," Richard said.

"I still got wet."

"It won't happen again. All I need you to do is hold the faucet in place while I attach it."

She looked at him wryly.

"I'll buy you dinner if you help me," he coaxed when she didn't respond.

Maggie felt anticipation surge through her at the thought of going out to dinner with Richard, of spending the evening with him. And afterward, they could go back to her place and . . . Her mouth began to water as images of exactly what she would like to do with him flashed through her mind.

No, she hastily clamped down on her imagination. She didn't know him well enough to invite him back to her apartment. He might look respectable, but looks could be deceptive. Look at her. New looks aside, she was as clueless about men as it was possible to be and still lay claim to femininity. But there was no reason to stay clueless. Not with Richard around . . .

The thought of Worthington and her plans for him briefly crossed her mind. Going out with Richard wouldn't jeopardize those plans, she assured herself. Richard was a plumber who happened to be doing some work in Worthington's apartment. It was highly unlikely that the two of them would even meet, let alone exchange confidences about the women they'd dated. Besides, going out with Richard would give her a chance to practice feeling comfortable around a man. She stole a quick glance at him and a shiver of awareness slithered down her spine. Somehow, *comfortable* and *Richard* were not mutually compatible concepts.

"It's a deal," she accepted, hoping the eagerness she felt wasn't apparent in her voice. "I'll help you plumb and then we can have dinner." Never mind the work back at the office she was completely blowing off. Another reaction that wasn't like her.

It didn't take long to hook up the faucet, and Maggie stepped back with a pleased smile on her face when water gushed out with no sign of leakage. "I can see where you'd like plumbing. When you're finished, you see positive results."

"Most jobs are like that."

"Not always," she said ruefully. "I like my job, but sometimes I can work for days chasing a bug and still have nothing to show for it."

"What exactly do you do?" Richard asked, curious as to what her role was in the company.

"Mostly, I liaison with customers, helping them figure out what they want and what kind of program can best help them do it. Sam Moore, our ex-president, used to say he sold the idea and it was up to me to translate it into something practical."

Richard felt a slight chill at the warmth in her voice as she mentioned Moore. Just how friendly was she with Moore? Obviously friendly enough to resent his no longer being there. But had she been friendly enough to know what he'd been up to? The thought jarred, and he shoved it to the back of his mind because there was no way he could answer it now. He'd have a better picture of what the situation was after the computer-fraud expert had done his work. Until then, he'd assume

Maggie was exactly what she seemed to be: a gorgeous, sexy woman who found him interesting.

"And do you make it practical?" he asked.

"About ninety-nine percent of the time. I find programming fascinating, but then I'm a bit of a computer fanatic." Maggie kept her answer brief for fear of boring him. As more than one of her girlfriends had told her, not everyone was as interested in computer applications as she was.

"What time do you want to eat?" she asked.

Richard checked the gold watch on his wrist and Maggie frowned slightly as she noticed it. It was an odd watch for a plumber to have. She would have expected him to own something in stainless steel with lots of gadgets. Instead, he was wearing a thin dress watch that didn't appear to do anything other than tell time.

"Seven?" he suggested. "How about if I get a couple of tickets to a Broadway show for after dinner?"

"No." Maggie hastily refused his offer. She wanted to spend the evening talking and getting to know him and she could hardly do that if they were at a performance. It would be better to keep the first date unstructured so that she could cut it short if the pressure got to be too much for her.

"You don't like live theater?" he asked curiously.

"Yes, but it's been a long week and I'm tired," she improvised. "I'd probably fall asleep in a darkened theater."

"Okay, I'll pick you up at seven. What's your address?"

"How about if I meet you in front of the restaurant?" Maggie remembered her earlier reservations about giving out her home address to a stranger. Even a fascinating stranger.

"Do you have a favorite?"

"There's a good restaurant over by the Museum of Natural History that serves an excellent blackberry salmon," Maggie said.

"What's the name of the place?"

Maggie searched her memory and came up blank. "I can't remember. How about if I meet you in front of the museum. The entrance that faces the park?"

Richard squashed the spurt of anger he felt at her refusal to trust him with her address. This wasn't San Francisco, he reminded himself. New York apparently had its own set of dating rules. Besides, he thought with satisfaction, one phone call to personnel on Monday and he'd have her file, complete with her home address. He could wait until then.

"The entrance in front of the park," he repeated.

"Did Romanos say when his boss was due in?" she asked.

"No, he didn't say much of anything. He just left some papers and took that folder you brought."

Maggie frowned slightly.

"What's the matter?" he asked, wondering if she would make an excuse to go back into the study to look at the papers Daniel had left.

"Did you ask to see any ID? I saw Romanos in the office so I'd recognize his face, but you wouldn't know him," she added at Richard's blank look. "All jokes about industrial spying aside, our company does some highly sensitive work for some pretty high-powered financial institutions."

Richard resisted the urge to reassure her, knowing that the only way he could was to admit he was Worthington, and he didn't want to do that until he'd had a chance to get to know her. And for her to get to know him. "Was there something confidential in what you brought?" he said.

"I don't actually know but probably not.

47

If it *had* been highly confidential, Emily would have brought it herself." At least, she hoped Emily would have been professional enough to put aside her animosity long enough to do it.

"I'll see you at seven, and thanks for your help with the faucet," Richard said as he walked her to the door.

"You're welcome." Maggie stepped out into the hallway and heard the door close behind her with a restrained thud. The flash of loss she felt at the sound caught her off guard. She'd just met the man, for heaven's sake. She couldn't miss him already.

Stepping into the elevator, she automatically pushed the button for the lobby. Her mind was fully occupied with trying to make sense of her unusual reaction to Richard. She couldn't. She had no idea why her response to him had been so strongly sensual. Granted, he was gorgeous, but gorgeous men were a dime a dozen in a city the size of New York. It was as if her emotions had recognized him on some level that her rational mind didn't even know existed.

She gave Emily a quick call to let her know she wouldn't be returning to work and then made her way to the front entrance. She shivered as she stepped out of the apartment building and a cool gust of spring wind pounced on her, making her damp sweater feel cold and clammy. She hurried toward the bus stop. She needed to get home and into dry clothes before she came down with something.

Thirty minutes later, she let herself into her apartment and, after making herself a cup of apricot coffee, powered up her computer, bringing up her dating program. She hadn't learned as much as she'd hoped about Worthington from her visit to his apartment, but every little bit helped. The more facts she entered, the more accurate the responses would be when she asked it questions.

Maggie caught her lower lip between her teeth as she wondered what kinds of things the program would tell her if she had a way to use it on Richard.

On the other hand, it might be more fun to delve into Richard's personality the old-fashioned way. Slowly. Taking her time to learn his likes and dislikes. Discovering all the little quirks that made him the unique individual he was. A shiver ran over her skin at the thought. She didn't have the slightest doubt that it would be worth every second it took.

The chime of her clock reminded her of the passing time, and she hurriedly finished keying in the information about Worthington's apartment. The information she had garnered so far about what made John Worthington tick was still sketchy at best, she thought with frustration. Hopefully, that would improve once she actually met the man and was able to observe him in action. Then she could fine tune her program, and begin to ask it questions more complicated than what his ideal woman looked like and how he would respond to general situations.

A sense of anticipation mixed with dread roiled through her at the thought of using it. Anticipation over Worthington being held accountable for his ruthlessness. Dread of the possible consequences of her actions, of setting events in motion that might be hard to control.

Wealthy men tended to think of themselves as outside the normal rules of civilized behavior. Her one and only meeting with her biological father had graphically proved that to her. And, according to her research, Worthington was far wealthier than her father had been.

But even if she failed in her attempts to make Worthington pay, it couldn't backfire, could it? She tried to look at the situation logically. He couldn't hurt her emotionally. She would never be dumb enough to fall for the guy. Not only did she have good reason to dislike Worthington personally but also her mother's experience had taught her to avoid wealthy men like the plague. Besides, her intense attraction to Richard was almost like being inoculated against John Worthington. No, emotionally she was safe.

And what else could he realistically do to her? Fire her? That didn't matter because she fully intended to leave just as soon as she found another job anyway. She didn't want to work for a man who treated his employees the way Worthington had treated Sam.

A second chime from the clock galvanized her into action and she hurried to get ready.

Once she had showered and liberally sprayed herself with the light floral scent she preferred, she hurried into the bedroom to get dressed.

Opening her closet, she automatically grabbed one of her pre-Worthington outfits. Catching herself, she hastily put it back. Like the rest of her old wardrobe, it was in earth tones and bought two sizes too big to successfully disguise the shape of her breasts and the curve of her hips. It was designed to make men's eyes skim over her without lingering.

A shudder of distaste churned through her stomach as she remembered the feel of her first foster father's eyes on her. Remembered the feeling of contamination, as if her body were somehow responsible for his licentious thoughts and the whispered filth he'd subjected her to every time he'd caught her alone.

That wasn't your fault, she said to herself, slicing off the insidious memories. He was the archetypal dirty old man, but that was *his* problem, not *yours,* Maggie reminded herself, remembering what the psychologist had told her. Her mind might believe it, but somehow her intellect had never been able to convince her emotions. Every time a man looked at her, she didn't see honest appreciation of her femininity; she saw unclean lust.

Face it, woman, she told herself. *You allowed a dirty old man to dictate your relationship to your feelings for the past fourteen years, and it's long past time to stop it!*

She nodded decisively. Getting revenge on Worthington would serve a dual purpose. Beyond the obvious one, it would be the opportunity to learn to dress so that she looked like what she wanted to be inside — a thoroughly modern professional. And after she'd finished with Worthington, maybe she could hang up her emotional baggage in the back of the closet with her unflattering wardrobe. Maybe she could risk looking for someone to share her life with. There had to be some men out there who would enrich her life instead of hopelessly complicating it. All she had to do was to find one.

A shiver of pleasure skittered over her skin as an image of Richard filled her mind. What would it be like to wake up in the morning next to him? The intriguing question crossed her mind. On the surface, Richard seemed like he could be the ideal man for her. He was built like the living embodiment of every sexual fantasy she'd ever had. He was easy to talk to, with a sense of humor that appealed to her, and he was perfect financially.

The sound of the clock as it struck half past the hour jerked her out of her thoughts. If she didn't hurry up, she'd be late, and he might not wait.

After dressing, she grabbed a cab. She had the driver drop her off a block from the museum so that she could casually walk up. She didn't want Richard to think she had been standing around, waiting for him.

To her relief, Richard was already there when she arrived. She paused slightly behind a woman pushing a double baby stroller and studied him as he stared out into the street, clearly waiting for a taxi to pull up.

Compulsively, her eyes ran over him. He was wearing a pair of cream chinos, a pale blue T-shirt and a white linen jacket that made his shoulders seem even broader. His dark hair was slightly disheveled from the wind and her fingertips tingled with a compulsion to touch it.

Richard turned, tensing when he caught sight of her. He felt the impact of her presence in every cell of his body. On the way over he'd told himself that his memory had exaggerated her appeal, but clearly it hadn't. He still found her physically fascinating. She drew him in on some instinctive level that totally bypassed rational thought.

Okay, so he was sexually attracted to her. There was nothing wrong with that. He was a free adult male. There was no reason for him not to explore that attraction. Especially considering that his interest had to be reciprocated or she wouldn't have accepted his invitation to dinner. And she'd accepted it without knowing who he really was. Normally, he never knew if a woman liked him or his considerable bank balance, but with Maggie, he knew he didn't have to wonder. She didn't have a clue as to his net worth and she still wanted to go out with him. He was looking forward to the novel experience of just being an average man.

"Hi," she said when she reached him.

"Good evening." He took her arm and started down the steps toward the street.

"Did Worthington show before you left?" she asked.

"No one came before I left," he said honestly.

A block away from the museum, he paused in front of a restaurant. "Is this the place you were talking about?"

"No, I've never been here." She read the menu posted beside the door and barely suppressed a wince. There were no prices listed.

"See anything you like?"

Maggie stared blankly at the menu as she tried to decide what to do. Business lunches with clients had taught her that restaurants that didn't post their prices were expensive. Very expensive. And she most emphatically didn't want Richard to remember their date as one that had cost him an arm and a leg. On the other hand, she didn't want to imply that he couldn't afford it. If the dating articles she'd read were right, men tended to have surprisingly fragile egos when it came to money.

To her relief, Richard provided the answer himself. "Don't you like French cuisine?" he asked.

"No," Maggie lied without a qualm. "They eat some very strange parts of animals, and I'm always worried about what might show up in a sauce. That place I mentioned is only a little farther and it's . . ." She scrambled to come up with an acceptable synonym for *cheaper* and failed.

Richard stared at her with a feeling of unreality as he suddenly realized what the problem was. She was actually worried about what this place would cost. He couldn't ever remember any woman trying to save him money. On the contrary, they were usually trying to separate him from large chunks of it.

Should he tell her who he really was now? That would certainly take care of her worries. But it would also change the way she responded to him, and he was enjoying being treated like a normal man too much. Not only that but also he needed more time to convince her that he wasn't the ogre that office gossip had painted him.

No, he'd stick to his original plan and tell her his real identity when the evening was over, he finally decided. After he'd thoroughly kissed her good-night.

Chapter Three

"Here's that place I mentioned," Maggie said.

Richard peered inside. It was only half-full, so getting a table wouldn't be a problem. "Looks good to me," he said.

Opening the door, he ushered her inside. The man at the bar gestured them toward the tables, and Maggie chose one well away from the door so that she wouldn't get hit with cool air every time it opened.

"May I get you something to drink?" The waitress who had materialized by their table was staring at Richard as if she'd suddenly hit the jackpot.

"A glass of white wine," Maggie said, feeling a gust of anger when the woman's attention never wavered from Richard. She wanted to post a sign on him that said Taken — Keep Your Hands Off! And Eyes, Too. Maggie watched the waitress literally devour him with her gaze.

But to Maggie's surprise, Richard didn't even seem to notice the woman's obvious interest. Was it because he was so used to attracting feminine attention or because he had the good manners not to flirt with one woman while he was out with another? She didn't know, and it was hardly the kind of question she could ask. It would appear that there were some pitfalls to dating a fabulous-looking man, she thought. But in Richard's case, it was worth it.

After the waitress had brought their drink orders, Maggie stole a quick look at Richard over the rim of her glass of wine. He was eating the appetizers the waitress had left with a single-minded concentration that bespoke imminent starvation.

A twinge of tenderness flashed through her at his absorbed expression. He was so gorgeous, and yet he seemed totally unaware of his looks. Was it normal for a man to be that oblivious to his physical appearance? She didn't have enough experience to tell. She'd only had one date with a man who couldn't even approach Richard for looks, and that had been a total disaster.

The man had been a coworker who, after ignoring her for the six months he'd been with the company, had suddenly asked her out. She'd spent the incomprehensible concert on modern music he'd taken her to trying to figure out why. She'd found out afterward when he'd mentioned, with elaborate casualness, that he had this design problem with his program and asked if she could help him solve it.

Strangely, finding out that he only wanted to use her hadn't even hurt that much because the whole evening had had a surrealistic feel to it. As if he were some celluloid character from a bad movie who had been temporarily animated.

Richard glanced up and asked, "Why the pensive look?"

"Just thinking," she muttered as she frantically searched her memory for something to say. Something that would capture his interest and convince him that, if she wasn't exactly a brilliant conversationalist, she was, at least, a passable one. A sense of frustration filled her as her mind refused to come up with a single idea from all those articles on dating that she'd consumed for the purpose of fascinating Worthington, if she could ever get him to ask her out.

Finally, one bit of advice rose to the surface of her muddled thoughts. People, be they men or women, liked to talk about themselves, so ask a leading question.

"What made you go into plumbing?" she blurted out. It might not be scintillating conversation, but it was a start. Anything was better than a pregnant silence.

A flush of heat poured through her at the thought of pregnancy of any kind. Of being in Richard's strong arms. Of being held close to his broad chest. Of . . .

"My father was in construction and he got me my first job when I was thirteen." Richard told her the absolute truth. His father *was* in construction. He owned one of the biggest firms on the West Coast, and from the time Richard had turned thirteen, his father had demanded that he earn all his spending money by working on various construction projects in the Bay Area.

"Thirteen?! That was awfully young to be around all that heavy equipment."

"Illegal, too." Richard chuckled. "I used to have to disappear when the building inspectors showed up."

"You could have been hurt." The very idea appalled her. What kind of man would allow his son to do anything like that? Apparently, one who was no more caring than her own father had been.

"It wasn't dangerous. I worked on one-story homes. Dad took good care of me."

Maggie heard the very real affection in his voice. Not like her father, she thought, changing her mind.

"Dad was a great believer in work ethic, and it certainly didn't do me any harm.

Didn't your father make you work for your spending money?"

Richard watched in surprise as her mobile features suddenly seemed to ice over. Why? he wondered. Because of the question itself or because he'd mentioned her father?

"My father died eighteen months ago," Maggie said stiffly as the memory of that last humiliating visit from his lawyer replayed itself in her mind. She took a deep, steadying breath and slowly exhaled, shoving the memory back into her subconscious, where it belonged.

"I'm sorry," he said softly.

Reaching across the table, he covered her slight hand with his much larger one.

Maggie tensed as the heat from his fingers seeped into her rigid muscles and surged along her nerve endings, momentarily short-circuiting her thoughts. Images of her father faded like mist hit by the midday sun. Richard's hand tightened comfortingly for a second before he removed it.

Maggie locked her muscles against her instinctive urge to grab his hand back. To carry it to her cheek and rub it over her skin. To press a kiss in his palm. She stared for a moment at the pristine whiteness of the tablecloth as she struggled to get her feelings under control. She might not know much about men, in general, but she knew enough to know that most men would run a mile from any excessive emotionality. Especially from someone they just met. She absolutely had to play it cool until she knew him better.

"My mother died sixteen years ago and I still miss her," Richard said softly. "But in time, you'll find the grief fades and they become a loving memory to warm you."

Maggie gave him a shaky smile, knowing she couldn't tell him the truth: that she didn't have loving memories of either parent. Telling him the truth might make him wonder if there was something wrong with her that made it impossible for her own parents to love her.

Richard mentally cursed himself for inadvertently upsetting her. He wanted to wipe out the pain he could see in her eyes, and yet bitter experience had taught him that there were no magic words to make everything better.

He changed the subject. "Do you have any siblings?"

"Nope. I'm an only child." Maggie leaned back as the waitress arrived with their dinner. Once the meal had been served, she asked, "How about you?"

"Also an only child. And I hated it. It

was lonely and there was no one to blame anything on. My parents always knew who'd been the one to get in trouble because I was the only candidate. I always wanted to have half a dozen kids, but since I don't intend to marry until I'm at least fifty, I guess I'll have to settle for four," he added deliberately. He might find Maggie intriguing, and he might be hoping that she'd help him fill his leisure hours over the next six weeks, but he had no intention of lying to accomplish it. She needed to understand up front that marriage was the furthest thing from his mind.

"Half a dozen?!" Maggie blinked, a forkful of food suspended halfway to her mouth. "Do you know what the average kid costs to raise?"

"No, do you?"

"Last time I saw a figure, it was pushing a quarter of a million, and that's just money."

"Just money?" he repeated, curious as to her choice of words.

"In one sense, money is the easiest thing to give kids," she said earnestly, remembering how her own father's total involvement in her life had been to send a monthly check through his lawyer for her maintenance. "Average parents both work, so they don't have much free time. How would you divide that little time among six kids?"

"When I was growing up, my best friend had seven kids in his family and his parents seemed to do a good job."

"Einstein did a great job on the theory of relativity, but that doesn't mean that anyone else could."

"That is a specious argument!"

"True." She grinned at him. "But I'm sure there's a point buried there somewhere."

"Probably several and none of them relevant since I'm not considering fatherhood in the foreseeable future."

Maggie squashed her annoyance that he felt it necessary to warn her twice within the space of minutes not to view him as a potential husband. Nor was she going to agonize over whether she might have inadvertently done or said something to give him the idea that she had marriage in mind. Maybe it was just that his last girlfriend had started pushing for more than he'd been willing to give.

Or was he presently involved with someone? The appalling thought occurred to her. She might not date much, but that didn't mean she was naive. Just because he'd asked her out didn't mean he was free to do so.

She decided to simply ask. "I take it you aren't presently in a relationship." It didn't seem like an unreasonable question to ask a man who'd invited her out.

Richard spared a brief thought to the supermodel he'd broken up with shortly before he'd left San Francisco. But calling their association "a relationship" was giving it depth beyond its just desserts. They had had an affair — period. There had been no emotional involvement for either of them.

"No," he said. "What about you?"

"Also, no. I've been much too busy establishing my career to invest much time in a relationship," she said, hoping that he would take that to mean that she wasn't the type of woman to view every man she ran across as a potential husband.

"Your career is important to you?" he asked.

"Yes." Her absolute sincerity was unmistakable. Thanks to her career, she would never again be at the mercy of forces she couldn't influence, let alone control. No one was ever going to make her do anything she didn't want to do or go anywhere she didn't want to go again.

Richard relaxed slightly at the fervor in her voice. Anyone that enthusiastic about her job would not be looking to change his bachelor status.

She drove the point home. "I really like my job. At least I did." Anger filled her at the realization that everything would change when Worthington took over on Monday.

As the busboy cleared away their dishes, Richard watched the emotions flittering across her expressive features and wondered what she was thinking. Was she worried about her job now that the company had been sold? Maybe he should reassure her about her future in the company now. He'd intended to tell her his real identity at the end of the evening anyway.

Much as he was enjoying being just plain Richard without the baggage of his wealth and social position muddying the waters, he was finding it harder and harder to deceive her. She was so open and honest that he wanted to match her.

Tell her now, he ordered himself. *Get it over with and you can both have a good laugh about the misunderstanding and then go on to spend the rest of the evening somewhere else.* Somewhere a little more private, where he could take her in his arms and . . . He hastily cut off the line of thought. First, he needed to clear the deck of misunderstandings, then he could make a move on her.

He accepted the cup of coffee the waitress offered him and stared down into the dark liquid as he tried to decide how to phrase his confession.

What was going on? Maggie wondered uneasily. All of a sudden, Richard looked . . . implacable, she decided with a shiver. Like a judge just before he handed out a harsh sentence.

Richard forced the words out. "Umm, I need to tell you something."

Maggie tensed at the flatness of his tone. Please don't let him say he forgot to mention that he's married, she frantically prayed.

"My full name is John Richard Worthington."

"John Worthington?" Maggie repeated blankly as his words ricocheted through her brain, numbing her mind and dulling her responses.

"But you aren't supposed to be in New York yet," she finally said. "Emily specifically said you weren't flying in until later tonight. Why would you give me a fake name, and what were you doing fixing the plumbing?"

Richard chose to answer the easiest question first. "I was fixing the plumbing because I wanted to move in and the janitor was off sick today. It was easier to do it myself than find a plumber on short notice. The guard in the lobby loaned me the janitor's tools. As for your other questions, I was able to get an earlier flight at the last minute, and I didn't give you a fake name — at least, not intentionally. My father is also named John, so I've always been known by my middle name."

"You deliberately let me think you were the plumber!" she bit out as anger began to nudge confusion aside. It didn't seem possible that the man she was so attracted to was actually John Worthington. One thing was certain, she thought furiously. She no longer had to wonder if the stories of his ruthlessness were exaggerated. She knew firsthand that they weren't.

She focused on feeding her anger, trying to ignore her underlying sense of loss. As if something precious that she'd momentarily had within her grasp had suddenly been snatched away.

"I wanted to give you time to realize that I'm not the monster that office gossip is making me out to be. Maggie, don't overreact."

Richard grabbed her hand. The slightly roughened skin of his fingers scraped across her skin, and she shivered.

Maggie stared down at their joined hands in disbelief. How could she still want him when he'd lied to her? It made no sense. The knowledge of his duplicity should have instantly killed her longing for him. So why hadn't it? It was still as strong as it had ever been, and that made her even angrier. She felt as if everything was conspiring against her, even her own body.

She looked at him and her anger was momentarily suspended at the concern she could see in his eyes. He did empathy well. She mocked her longing to believe it was real.

All her life, she'd had to endure what people in positions of authority had thrown at her because she'd been powerless, but she wasn't powerless now. Thanks to her program, she had a secret weapon. She had knowledge, and knowledge could change worlds. It might even be able to put a dent in an ego the size of John Richard Worthington's.

But first, she needed to get control of the confusing mix of emotions swirling through her.

Making a monumental effort, she forced

a level tone. "I'm not overreacting. I'm just surprised, that's all."

Richard studied her tense features, which were at odds with her calm voice. Had she forgiven him, or had she just decided that it wouldn't be too bright to make an enemy of the man who owned the company that employed her? He didn't know, but he would find out, he vowed. During the six weeks he'd be here, he intended to learn everything there was to know about Maggie, including what it was like to make love to her.

But first, he had to regain the ground he'd lost by his confession. He needed to get her thinking of him as Richard again, to reestablish the easy sense of camaraderie that they'd had earlier.

But what could they do for the rest of the evening? Certainly nothing to do with work. That would only reinforce who he really was. No, he needed something to fill the rest of the evening that . . .

An idea occurred to him when he remembered something he'd read in the paper that afternoon. Something about a diamond exhibit over at the Met. He'd never met a woman yet who wasn't interested in diamonds.

Maggie would feel safe because they

would be in a public place with a crowd around, a crowd of people going about their own concerns, allowing him to carry on a private conversation with her and repair the damage done by revealing his identify. It was perfect.

"How about if we stop by the Met to see that exhibit on diamonds they're showing?" he suggested, hoping he sounded more casual than he felt. Letting her know just how strongly he was attracted to her would be a bad tactical error because that would give her power. And bitter experience had taught him that when a woman had sexual power, she always used it to a man's disadvantage.

Maggie was torn by his throwaway tone. Her pride demanded that she refuse and leave, but her common sense told her to accept. Her plan for revenge depended on Richard falling for her, and he couldn't do that if she weren't around. From what she'd been able to learn about him, she very much doubted that he'd bother to chase her. He was so spoiled for choice when it came to women that he'd probably simply shrug and move on to the next available one. Her heart seemed to skip a beat at the thought of never seeing him again or, even worse, of only seeing him in a formal business setting.

She was swallowing her pride for Sam's sake, she told herself. For once in her life, she was going to make sure that the people who held power were also held accountable for the grief they caused by the capricious use of that power.

And as for her fledgling feelings for Richard, the plumber, they had died the minute she'd found out that there wasn't such a person, she assured herself. All that was left now was a basic physical attraction that would quickly fade because she was far too smart to ever get mixed up with a man of his wealth. A man who changed his women as often as she changed her clothes. In a very real sense, her whole life had been a warning of the dangers of playing around with men who didn't even acknowledge the rules that governed normal people.

She was going to thoroughly enjoy teaching Worthington a lesson. This was going to be a six weeks he'd never forget.

She reached for a mildly interested tone and landed on wooden instead. "That sounds nice, I've been meaning to see it."

Richard relaxed slightly at her acceptance. He knew she hadn't entirely forgiven him for his deception — that was clear by the tone of her voice — but she wasn't so angry that she was willing to cut him out of her life. All he had to do was get on her good side again by letting her discover who he was. It shouldn't be too hard, he thought cynically. There wasn't a woman alive who would prefer a plumber to a billionaire businessman once she'd had time to think about it.

Outside the restaurant, Richard hailed a cab, which obediently pulled over to the curb. Opening the back door, he put a hand on the small of her back to guide her into the taxi. He'd be glad when his normal driver arrived from San Francisco the week after next. He missed both the privacy and the convenience of having Edward drive him. Even so, he hadn't had the heart to tell him he was needed in New York at once. Not when the man was counting down the days until his daughter gave birth to his first grandchild. He just hoped the kid took after Edward and wasn't late.

Maggie tensed slightly and hastily scooted across the vinyl seat. How could she possibly feel his touch through her clothes? she wondered uneasily.

She couldn't, she assured herself. All she was doing was reacting to his overabundance of sexual charisma. And all that proved was that she was a perfectly normal woman with perfectly normal sexual reactions when faced with one of nature's more spectacular male creations.

She found her gaze dropping to his thighs and a surge of warmth engulfing her as she wondered if he was as big all over.

Her unsettling daydream was rudely interrupted as the cabbie executed a U-turn with a tire-squealing shriek and raced back the way he had come.

Not having had time to fasten her seat belt, Maggie slid across the seat and landed against Richard's hard body. It was like hitting a concrete wall. A warm concrete wall that smelled exactly like the flowering lemon grove she'd visited in Tuscany last spring.

She took a breath, drawing the tantalizing aroma deeper into her lungs. He smelled so good. Fresh and clean and outdoorsy. And overwhelmingly sexy.

He's also a ruthless tycoon who destroyed Sam's career, she thought, forcing herself to remember what lay beneath his enticing exterior.

"We aren't in that much of a hurry," Richard told the cabbie, and the man obediently slowed down.

He had the most fantastic voice. Deep

and dark and velvety. It made her think of long, steamy nights spent among tangled sheets. If there had been any justice in the world, he should have had a high, squeaky voice just to balance out his other physical attributes, she thought ruefully. But apparently, the good fairies had been out in full force at Richard's christening. He had it all. Except for compassion, she reminded herself. And common decency or he wouldn't have treated Sam so appallingly. It was just that what he lacked wasn't readily apparent to the naked eye.

The word *naked* immediately brought to mind the memory of Richard's bare chest, and her breath shortened with longing.

Stop it! she ordered her unruly emotions. You have a goal, and it doesn't include jumping into bed with him.

Chapter Four

The driver pulled up in front of the Met with a bone-jarring application of the brakes, and Maggie hastily climbed out of the cab, trying to escape as much from her own thoughts as from the driver's homicidal driving tendencies.

"New York taxi drivers are one thing that never changes," Richard said as he joined her on the steps of the Met.

"Unfortunately," Maggie said wryly.

She followed Richard into the museum and was about to pull out her pass when Richard put down the money for two admissions. Let him pay, she decided. He could certainly afford it.

Richard looked up from the floor plan of the museum he was studying and remarked, "It says here that they have suits of armor."

"Of course, they do. The Met isn't just any art museum," she said with the pride of a native New Yorker.

"It is *the* American art museum."

"Would you mind if we took a quick look at those first?" Richard asked.

"Sure, we have time to see both exhibits before the museum closes. What period of armor are you interested in?"

"Any period. As a kid, I was fascinated by King Arthur and his knights. My burning goal was to somehow figure out a way to time-travel and join them. I must have read *A Connecticut Yankee in King Arthur's Court* a dozen times."

"I suppose a kid might enjoy the Middle Ages."

"You don't like that time period?" he asked curiously.

"What was to like? Medicine was at the level of beads and chanting — the beads being rosary beads and the chanting being prayers — food was scarce and contaminated, and justice, when it existed, was administered at the whim of the local lord."

"Not a very romantic view."

"It wasn't a very romantic age," she said.

"What about Guinevere and Lancelot?" Richard argued, remembering how one of his girlfriends had dragged him to a movie about them and then spent the rest of the night rhapsodizing about their doomed love.

"What about them?" Maggie said. "Guinevere was married to Arthur, which makes her great love for Lancelot adultery."

Pain colored her voice as echoes of her mother defending her affair with Maggie's very much married father as true love welled out of her subconscious.

"If you're married to someone and it doesn't work out, then get a divorce and get on with your life. But Guinevere wanted the best of both worlds. She wanted the prestige and security of being queen, along with the excitement of a younger lover."

"I see," Richard said, taken aback at the obvious strength of her feelings. Most of the people he knew viewed adultery on a par with cheating on your income tax. Technically wrong, but everyone did it. But there had been nothing lukewarm about Maggie's reaction. It had been personal. Painfully personal.

Had she been drawn into an affair with a married man and then ditched? Or had her lover lied about being free and she hadn't found out he was married until after she'd been with him? Richard felt his muscles tense at the thought of someone taking sexual advantage of Maggie.

"The armor is through here." She headed through the museum shop and Richard forced himself to relax as he followed her. Clearly, she had no intention of explaining why she felt the way she did. Unlike most of the women he'd dated, Maggie was proving to be remarkably reticent about herself.

"You sure do take the bloom off history," Richard said.

"That's because I see the world the way it is not the way I want it to be."

"Is there much of a difference?"

"What do you mean?"

"Is there much of a disparity between the way the world is and the way you want it to be?"

The thought of her mother's emotionally destructive lifestyle and its tragic consequences crossed Maggie's mind, and her features tightened.

"No, don't answer that." Richard caught her flash of pain. He didn't want to remind her of anything unhappy. He wanted her to enjoy the evening with him, not relive bad memories.

"Ah, here we are. The armor," she said as they entered a room filled with glass cases.

"Fascinating —" Richard studied the suit of armor in the case in front of him "— but surprising."

Maggie looked at the shiny, silver armor and asked, "How so? It looks like a pretty standard suit to me."

"The size." Richard gestured toward it. "The man who wore that had to have been over six feet tall. I thought people were smaller in the past?"

"I hadn't noticed, but you're right. It is pretty big," she said as she examined the armor more closely. "I don't know for sure, but I would imagine that their short stature was more a result of bad nutrition than genetics. Maybe the guy who originally owned it simply drank his milk when he was a kid."

"He also had to do something to grow muscles strong enough to support the weight of all that metal. And he had to swing that weapon. I wonder how heavy it is." Richard eyed the sword lying on the floor of the case. "It must be four feet long."

"Chances are, it's made of good, solid Toledan steel. Believe me, it's heavy. The Society for the Preservation of Anachronisms down in southern Pennsylvania puts on an Elizabethan fair every year and I've gone a couple of times. One of the exhibits included armor and swords. I picked a sword up and had to use both hands to swing it. It's hard to imagine anyone actually using one while riding on the back of a horse and wearing armor."

81

"Those old knights must have been tremendous athletes," Richard said.

Maggie giggled.

"What's so funny?"

"I was just thinking of all those knights traipsing off to work out at the gym."

Richard grinned at the image her words evoked. She was so different from the women he usually dated. Normally, women fell all over themselves to impress him. Maggie seemed to operate from a "this is who I am, take it or leave it" mode. And he most definitely wanted to take her — at least for the six weeks he'd be in New York.

"For someone who isn't interested in the Middle Ages you sure know a lot about it."

"Not particularly. I just read a lot. I think the historical period I like best is the Regency period in England. I discovered Georgette Heyer when I was a teenager and her books made a big impression on me."

Richard frowned, trying to place the era and failing. It gave him an odd feeling not to be able to contribute meaningfully to the conversation. He hadn't realized it before, but in the past ten years, his interests had pretty much narrowed to business and situations that impacted on business, such as world politics and economic conditions. Even his social life hadn't expanded his horizons much because he hadn't talked to his dates about anything substantive. He hadn't gone out with them for their minds any more than they had been interested in his. They'd wanted his money and he'd wanted . . .

"Why don't we go see the diamond exhibit now?" he said, uncomfortable with his line of thought.

"If you're sure you're finished with the armor. We have plenty of time."

And he knew how he'd prefer to be spending that time, he thought. In bed. With Maggie. The Met might be turning out to be a lot more interesting than he'd expected, but even so, it couldn't compare with the thought of making love to her. But it was too soon. First, he had to convince her that he wasn't the monster that everyone around the office thought. Then when she was comfortable with him again, he could make a serious move on her. He had six weeks, he reminded himself. That should be more than enough time to sate his fascination with her.

"I've seen enough for this visit." He checked his museum map to see where they should be going. "It says the diamond exhibit is up on the second floor in the front."

"They usually put the special exhibits up there." She fell in step beside him.

One flight of stairs and two corridors later, they arrived at the exhibit and slipped past the crowd at the entrance.

"There appears to be lots of interest in it," Richard observed.

"Precious stones do seem to have a fascination all their own." Her voice trailed off as she studied the ornate cover of Catherine the Great's Bible.

"Those don't even look like diamonds. They look like chunks of quartz that a kid might have in his collection."

Maggie read the plaque beside the display. "It says that they didn't have the ability to facet diamonds at that time."

"You have to wonder why they decided to decorate with them, then. They aren't very attractive, although the rubies and emeralds are certainly eye-catching."

"They certainly are," Maggie agreed. "I like something with a little color to it myself."

"You can still have a diamond if you like color." Richard pointed to the next display case. "Look at all the colors of diamonds. They even come in black."

84

Maggie leaned over the case. "It looks gray to me. I like that rose diamond, though."

"Nice," Richard agreed as he pictured the oversized stone set in a ring. The warmth of the pink would glow against the pale cream of her slender fingers.

He followed Maggie as she moved to the next exhibit. "Frederick the Great used diamonds as buttons," she said in awe.

"Frederick the Great was sartorially challenged, I'll bet you ten to one, he was short and fat."

Maggie grinned. "Most of them did seem to run to fat by the time they got a *'Great'* stuck after their names."

"Look at that!" she suddenly said.

Richard looked where Maggie was pointing and found himself staring at the biggest diamond ring he'd ever seen.

"Given to Elizabeth Taylor by Richard Burton," he read.

"Now *that* was some love affair," Maggie said.

"Didn't they wind up divorced?"

"Yeah, I think twice, but I'm not sure. It was before my time. But then they should never have married."

"Why not if they loved each other?" he asked, curious about how she viewed love and marriage. Most of the women he knew drew a clear distinction between the two. Love was where you found it, but marriage was only to be entered into if money was present.

"They were clearly incompatible, and as for being in love, I'm not sure exactly what that means." Involuntarily, her eyes strayed to his large body and a shiver chased over her skin. She sure knew what lust was, though, she thought ruefully. It was what she felt every time she saw him. She wanted to jump his bones and make mad, passionate love to him. She wanted to spend days exploring her sensuality with him. And the fact that she knew just how ruthless he really was under that fabulous exterior didn't matter to her emotions one bit. Which said *what* about her? she wondered uneasily.

"You've never been in love?" Richard asked incredulously. The women he knew were forever falling in and out of love. Hell, ninety percent of the women he dated claimed to love him.

"Nope, but I've been infatuated a few times."

Richard felt a flash of dark emotion momentarily color his thoughts. For some reason, he didn't want to think of her as being infatuated with some man. With some other man. He wouldn't mind if she were infatuated with him, he decided. In fact, the idea had a lot of appeal.

"How can you tell the difference between love and infatuation?" he finally asked when she didn't elaborate on her statement.

"Well, however one defines love, I think it would have to include an acceptance of the person as a whole — their good points and their bad. When you're infatuated, you can't see beyond the physical. Once that fades, there's nothing left and the relationship falls apart."

She could be right, Richard thought, remembering the course of several of his affairs that had gone from raging desire to acute boredom in a matter of weeks. He glanced speculatively at Maggie and felt hunger slam through him as he watched her run the tip of her tongue over her bottom lip. He suspected it would be a long time before her physical fascination faded for him.

But how did *she* view *him?* he wondered. Her natural reserve made it hard to accurately read her, but even so, he was sure she was attracted to him. He'd seen it in her eyes before she'd had any idea who he really was. And if the occasional side-long glances he'd caught her giving him were any indication, finding out his real identity hadn't killed her interest in him. But it had made her more . . . cautious, he finally decided. As if she weren't quite sure if it was safe to be attracted to him. So how did he go about convincing her that he was really harmless? With smoke and mirrors, he thought ruefully.

They were examining a display of diamonds that showed all the different ways the gems could be cut when the museum announced it would be closing in five minutes.

With a feeling of surprise at how quickly the evening had passed, Maggie obediently joined the other patrons, who were heading toward the exits. At least, she put one of her fears to rest. She had no trouble holding up her end of a conversation with him. He was surprisingly easy to talk to, whether he was being himself or his alter ego, the plumber.

"That was a really great exhibit. Thanks for bringing me," she told him.

"It was my pleasure," Richard said, realizing, to his surprise, that it really had been. He had enjoyed himself immensely, not so much viewing the exhibit as watching Maggie's reaction to it.

"Would you like to get a cup of coffee?" Richard asked.

Maggie squashed her instinctive urge to accept. Instead, she forced herself to remember her long-term goal. And to have any chance of doing that, she had to make herself stand out from his usual dates. Her program had been specific. Richard had a very short attention span when it came to women. He was quickly bored, so the only way to hold his interest long enough for him to fall for her would be to keep him guessing. And that meant she couldn't accept his every invitation. Just some of them.

"No, thanks," she said as they emerged into the cool night air. "I need to get back."

"Oh?" Richard's deep voice invited her to tell him why, but she didn't respond.

"I can catch a cab here," Maggie said as they emerged from the Met into the cool spring evening. She said good-bye and headed toward the line of cabs waiting to pick up the last of the museum patrons.

Resisting her compulsion to turn and take one last look at Richard, she forced herself to lean against the musty-smelling seat and assess her evening.

All in all, it wasn't a bad beginning, she decided. All the work she'd put into her program appeared to be paying off. Richard seemed to have taken the bait.

Actually, she'd be doing the rest of womankind a big favor, she told herself. Richard would be a much better person when she was done with him. So why didn't she feel better about what she planned to do, she wondered, but no answer came to mind.

Maggie studied herself critically in the full-length mirror on her closet door. The white hip-hugger pants and silk T-shirt fitted her perfectly. Granted, her breasts were a little too full for how slender she was — she tried to ignore the memory of her foster father's hateful voice telling her that she had the perfect hooker's body — but her stomach was flat thanks to all those sit-ups she did and her rear . . . She twisted slightly to view the body part in question, but it didn't stick out much, and her thighs didn't bulge anywhere. Her eyes followed the long, smooth length of her form-fitting pants.

A quick glance at the clock told her to hurry, and she grabbed the white blazer that went with the outfit and slipped it on, immediately feeling a little better now that she was a bit more covered up. She had plenty of time, but she didn't want to be late. Not for her yearly reunion with her three foster sisters.

She saw Jessie, who also lived in the city, a couple times a month, but Candice was a partner in an up-and-coming advertising agency in Chicago and Mary taught at Notre Dame in Northern Indiana. And while frequent e-mails and phone calls did keep them up-to-date with each others' lives, it wasn't nearly as satisfactory as talking in person.

She grimaced as she remembered the fear she'd felt eleven years ago when the social worker met with the four of them and told them that their foster parents were moving to Florida and that the system had decided to separate them. Remembered how angry and powerless the four of them had felt. They'd vowed to meet every year on the Saturday nearest to the date they'd been separated at Candice's favorite museum, the JP Morgan.

Grabbing her purse, she hurried out of her apartment to get a cab.

On her way to the museum, she briefly considered asking the driver to detour past Richard's apartment on the off chance that she might catch a glimpse of him, either coming or going, but common sense stopped her. If he was there and he caught sight of her, it could damage her campaign. The program had been very specific about Richard's dislike of being chased. And at this tentative stage of their relationship, she very much suspected that he would view cruising past his apartment as chasing.

Would he view her asking him out in the same light? She wondered. She decided to ask the program that evening.

Maggie released her breath in a long sigh. It made the cabbie give her a quizzical look that she missed. Her program sure took the fun out of dating. It made everything seem so calculated. But going out with Richard *wasn't* dating, she reminded herself. And she didn't dare forget it. Going out with Richard was revenge, pure and simple.

An image of Richard's dark features floated through her mind and a frisson of unease shivered down her spine. Revenge against him would never be simple. Dangerous, yes, but not simple. There was nothing simple about the man.

The cab stopped at the corner of Thirty-ninth and Madison and she scrambled out, her eyes quickly scanning the sidewalk.

"Maggie!" A husky voice called her name with real pleasure and she turned in the direction of the sound. Her eyes brightened as she took in the sight of two of her foster sisters.

"Jessie, Candice!" She rushed toward them and was enveloped in a group hug. "It's so good to see you. You look great."

"And *you* look spectacular!" Jessie studied Maggie's outfit with undisguised admiration. "I tried to wear an all-white suit once. It seemed to collect stains all by itself. How do you get away with it?"

Maggie giggled, feeling like a teenager again. "You simply have to frown at them and the spots run. They're really very shy."

"As I remember, you were, too," Candice said dryly.

Maggie simply grinned, inordinately pleased at the new image she was projecting. Maybe if enough people saw her as sexy and modern, she'd begin to believe it herself.

"Is Mary here?" Maggie took a quick glance around.

"She . . . Isn't that her?" Candice gestured toward the stunning woman getting out of a cab around the corner.

Jessie sighed. "It sure is. I swear if there were any justice in this world, she'd weigh two hundred pounds. Instead, she looks even thinner than she did last year."

Maggie waved when she caught Mary's eye. "I know what you mean. If she weren't so nice, it would be really easy to work up a major dislike where she's concerned."

Candice chuckled as the three of them hurried toward Mary. "Much good it would do you. Unless you come wrapped up in a mathematical formula, Mary wouldn't even notice. I consider myself lucky if she remembers to answer my e-mails within the same month."

"She's not that bad," Maggie said. "Although I will admit I'm always surprised when she remembers our yearly dates."

"Mary, you look like a million bucks," Candice said when they reached her.

"Literally," Maggie agreed.

Mary smiled and her bright green eyes glowed. "Thanks. It's really good to see you all."

"Let's go into the cafeteria and talk." Jessie automatically slipped into the role of leader she'd occupied during their high-school years. The other three followed her.

Once they had bought their coffee and were seated in the light-filled atrium, Candice said, "Anybody get engaged since

I last talked to you? How about a really hot date?"

Maggie held her tongue. They didn't come any hotter than Richard Worthington, but she didn't want to tell them about him because that would involve explanations that she didn't want to make.

"Forget hot," Jessie said, "I'd settle for a date — period."

"I wouldn't mind having a couple of kids," Mary announced, and the other three turned as one to stare at her in shock.

"Kids?" Maggie repeated. "You've never shown the slightest interest in anything but math and physics."

Mary hunched her slender shoulders. "Yes, but as Candice said, we're not getting any younger."

The four of them were silent a moment as they pondered the undeniable fact.

"Let's talk about something cheerful," Maggie said.

"We could find a sidewalk café and sit and rate the guys that walk by?" Candice suggested with a reminiscent grin.

"Remember our junior year of high school, when that pompous English teacher found our notebook of ratings and was trying to figure out what it meant?"

"Yeah, and Maggie told him it was the rating system we'd devised for Shakespeare's sonnets, and he believed us?"

The sound of their happy laughter caused heads to turn.

"Come on." Jessie stood up. "Let's go find some place to watch the wild life."

"I'd settle for a man with *any* kind of life," Candice said wistfully as they left.

An image of Richard's lean features flashed through Maggie's mind and she wondered what she would have to settle for when her quest for revenge was over. It was a sobering thought.

Chapter Five

Richard scrolled down the computer screen, frowning at the paucity of information he'd found in Maggie's personnel file. He frowned slightly, wondering if they kept additional information on employees anywhere else.

Unfortunately, there wasn't anyone he could ask on a Saturday night. He was the only person in the office. Even the cleaning crew had left.

He scrolled down farther and read her work evaluations. According to her immediate supervisor, she was hardworking, bright and innovative. There was also an addendum by Moore concerning projects she'd done with him. He had credited her with everything but being able to walk on water.

Richard leaned back and absently rubbed his right earlobe as he reread Moore's praise. That Maggie was an outstanding employee was clear by her supervisor's comments, but what had motivated Moore to use such over-the-top superlatives? Had he really been influenced by the caliber of her work, or was it something else entirely?

Richard shifted uneasily as he remembered that his forensic accountant, who had examined the books before they'd bought the company, had believed that Moore had had help in his embezzlement scheme. That someone with a great deal of computer expertise had juggled the accounts for him. And Maggie was arguably the company's most creative computer person. Could she have used that creativity to help Moore steal? From what Daniel had been able to discover, she had worked very closely with Moore on an almost daily basis. Were his glowing evaluations a partial payoff for her help in his embezzlement scheme?

Richard remembered her deep blue gaze and found it hard to believe. Her relationship with Moore had probably been simply work related. But if he was wrong . . .

If he was wrong, if she was the one who'd helped Moore steal, he'd find that out, too. And he wanted to do it sooner than later.

Richard reached for the phone and dialed her number, which he'd been calling at fifteen-minute intervals since early afternoon, reaching only her voice mail in the process.

The best way to find out what made Maggie tick was to spend some time with her. Some quality time. The thought brought an image of her lying naked on the middle of his pale blue sheets, her reddish brown curls spread over his pillow and her eyes gleaming with desire for him. She'd raise her arms in welcome and . . .

A sense of disorientation filled him when she answered the phone.

Stifling an impulse to demand to know where she had been all day and, more importantly, with whom, he said, "Good evening, Maggie. It's Richard Worthington."

Maggie's breath caught in her throat and warmth shot through her as the dark, velvety sound of his voice stroked across her nerve endings. She took a deep, sustaining breath, trying to control her skyrocketing heartbeat.

"Hi," she said. Her initial sense of triumph at the fact that he'd been interested enough in her new image to call her again was drowned by dismay at her intense reaction to him. In order to successfully pull off her plan, she was going to have to keep her wits about her, and that was going to be extremely difficult if her feelings became involved. Somehow, she was going to have to lure him deeper into an emotional trap and yet remain above it.

An image of her lying on Richard's magnificent chest, looking down into his lean face, filled her mind and she shifted restlessly in reaction. Concentrate! she ordered herself. This is the enemy. Remember what he did to Sam. He might look like the answer to a woman's every romantic fantasy, but he acted like the kind of man every mother warns her daughter against.

A wistful smile curved her lips. At least, every normal mother. *Her* mother probably would have found out his bank balance and told Maggie to hop into bed with him in the hopes of extracting a big payoff.

"Are you still there?" Richard's voice had developed an edge to it, and Maggie hastily shoved her memories aside and forced herself to pay attention.

"Yes, of course," she said, trying to inject a cool friendliness into her voice. She'd spent an hour this morning reviewing her data on him and had decided to present him with a slightly reserved approach in hopes that he wouldn't be able to resist breaking it down. She just wished she had a little more experience in handling men to call upon. *Strike that,* she thought ruefully.

She wished she had *a lot* more experience to call upon.

"I tried to get you earlier . . ." Richard's voice trailed off, giving her a chance to tell him where she'd been.

Maggie bit back her instinctive impulse to explain about her yearly get-together with her foster sisters. Every article she'd ever read about dating — and she'd read plenty, preparing for Richard — had stated that a little bit of mystery enhanced a relationship. And considering the way Richard seemed to go through women, she knew she was going to need every advantage she could come up with.

"I was out," Maggie finally said. "I just got back and haven't had a chance to check my messages yet."

"I didn't leave you one," Richard said, knowing that he hadn't left her one because then he wouldn't have had an excuse to keep calling her if he had. A message would have left the decision of whether to contact him or not in her court, and he wasn't sure what she would do. She seemed to enjoy his company last night. But he was also aware that she'd been a lot more enthusiastic before she found out who he really was. Afterward, she'd been a little politer and a lot less spontaneous. He could only hope that their visit to the Met had made a start of showing her that he wasn't anything like office gossip had depicted him. What he needed to do now was take her out again as soon as possible to reinforce the idea that he was just a normal man.

"I've got theater tickets for a show. How about if we catch it and have dinner afterward?"

Yes! Maggie felt a surge of excitement at his invitation. Her plan was working. The fish was nibbling at the hook. Now all she had to do was make sure he swallowed the bait, and then she could reel him in.

The sudden image of a gigantic shark rising out of the water toward her flashed across her mind, bringing a swirl of fear in its wake, but she hurriedly banished it. Richard Worthington might be a tyrant, but he wasn't omnipotent. Nor was he omniscient or he'd know what she was up to. She could handle him.

"I'd enjoy that." She kept her voice pleasantly neutral. "How about if I meet you at the theater?"

"What is this aversion you have to being picked up at home?" he snapped, his frustration at her lack of enthusiasm adding an edge to his voice. He wanted her to be looking forward to going out with him. Instead, she sounded as prim as a little girl thanking an adult for an outing she didn't want to go on but was too polite to refuse. But she had to want to go. He argued with his gut feeling that he was missing something vital. She was an adult. If she didn't want to attend the theater with him, she could simply say so.

Unless she was leery of turning him down because he was her employer? The thought gave him pause. Damm it, that was why he normally avoided dating the women who worked for him like the plague. But even being aware of the potential pitfalls, he didn't consider withdrawing his invitation for a minute. He wanted to know more about Maggie. He wanted to bask in the warmth of her smile and sharpen his wits against her razor-sharp intelligence. And he needed to keep tabs on her until he found out if she really was involved with Moore in the embezzlement scheme, he rationalized.

"Hey, what can I say," Maggie said. "I'm a product of my environment, and this *is* New York City."

"Keep talking. So far, I haven't heard a reason that makes sense."

"We probably don't have any bigger percentages of nutcases than any other city, but because it's so big, the actual number of them is rather formidable. A single woman who gives out her address to someone she doesn't know all that well is a fool. But there is no reason for you not to pick me up if you want to." Especially since he could find out where she lived from personnel on Monday in two minutes flat, she thought practically.

"Okay, I'll pick you up at six-thirty. Good-bye."

"Good-bye." Maggie thoughtfully put the phone down.

She was beginning to feel like she was faced with an obstacle course liberally laced with land mines. One false step and she could get blown to smithereens.

She glanced at the large, ornately framed mirror she'd hung over her couch in the vain hope that it would make the tiny room look larger. Her gaze lingered on her slim reflection, with every curve lovingly outlined by the stretchy, white gabardine fabric of her pants.

How did men view her now? Her personality hadn't changed. She was still very reserved and felt uncomfortable when men stared at her. Although, nowadays, what she felt was really a flicker of unease, not the panic-stricken sense of shame and fear that her first foster father's constant sexual harassment had caused.

It was progress, she guessed. But she wasn't sure that she welcomed it. Denying her sexuality and hiding behind oversized clothes had kept her safe from both her own emotions and men's lascivious thoughts. If she didn't date, she couldn't be used and discarded, like her mother. But now . . .

She frowned slightly as she remembered the incredulous stares she'd gotten from some of her male coworkers when she first unveiled her new image two weeks ago. And the number of them who had immediately asked her out — and not all of them had been single.

You are an adult woman in charge of your own life, she assured herself. *Just because men are attracted to you, you aren't obligated to do anything about it. All you have to do is refuse to play games. Or, at least, you can choose which games you want to play and with whom you want to play them.*

Maggie nodded decisively as she went to get ready for the evening.

Thirty minutes later, she stood in front

of her closet, trying to decide what to wear. Nothing too formal. Her lips curved in a rueful smile. That was good because she didn't own anything too formal. When she'd bought her new wardrobe for "Operation Revenge," as she had mentally dubbed it, she hadn't bothered to buy anything overly dressy because of the expense.

Thoughtfully, she studied her choices. Err on the side of underdressing rather than overdressing, she remembered from a story in a fashion magazine she'd read. The article had been accompanied by a picture of a gorgeous woman wearing designer clothes who looked like she'd never made a fashion faux pas in her life.

Maggie pulled out a black, silk chiffon skirt printed with enormous red roses. It had an asymmetrical handkerchief hem that hit her left leg three inches above the knee and dropped to midcalf on her right leg.

Maggie slipped it on, frowning slightly at the way the silky material hugged her slender hips before flaring out at the thighs. Fashionable. Maggie ignored her sense of unease at having her body so clearly outlined.

She rummaged through her bureau drawer and came up with a black, silk halter top that the saleswoman had assured her would go with anything. Maggie slipped it on, wincing at the way the deep décolletage exposed the curves of her breasts. She twisted around, checking in the mirror the way the back dipped almost to her waist.

It was impossible to wear a bra with it, and she stared closer at her image trying to decide if it was obvious from the front. She didn't think so, but even if Richard could tell, it didn't matter, she assured herself. He was much too sophisticated a man to indulge in wrestling matches in the backs of taxis. The feeling of regret the thought engendered faintly horrified her.

She slipped on a pair of cluster earrings made of sterling silver and cherry quartz and added a matching necklace in hopes that people would focus on the delicate beauty of Alex Woo's jewelry, not her breasts.

She carefully applied her makeup and brushed her shiny brown hair, letting the long curls caress her bare shoulders.

She turned her head, satisfied at the way the light reflected off the glitter on her cheekbones. Putting on makeup might be a lot of work, but it was kind of fun, too.

The buzzer sounded, telling her that

Richard was in the lobby, and she hurriedly jammed her small feet into a pair of black peep-toe slingbacks with three inch heels. She almost tripped as she hurried over to the bureau to get a black silk shawl to protect her from the air-conditioning in the theater.

She glared down at the unaccustomed height of her shoes. She'd be lucky if she didn't wind up breaking her neck in these things. Why couldn't the fashion have been for something comfortable, like her Rockport walking shoes?

Grabbing her small, black clutch, she hit the intercom button and said, "I'm on my way down," then cut the connection before he could respond.

Richard tensed as the elevator doors opened and Maggie emerged. His breath caught in his lungs as a surge of plain old lust hit him. She was wearing a stretchy black top that gave him a tantalizing glimpse of her breasts. A compulsion to slip his hand beneath her neckline and caress her engulfed him. He wanted to find out if her skin was as soft and silky as it looked.

He took a deep, steadying breath as he felt his body begin to react to his thoughts. Slow down, he told himself, trying to dampen his reaction. He was going to be here for six weeks. He didn't have to rush anything. He had time to savor her.

Maggie felt the muscles in her abdomen clench as she stepped out of the elevator and saw Richard standing outside the street doors. He looked fantastic in pale gray cotton pants, a pristine white cotton shirt and a black linen jacket.

She didn't know the first thing about male fashion, but she could recognize custom-tailoring when she saw it. And as far as she was concerned, he'd wasted his money, she thought as she unconsciously ran her tongue over her dry bottom lip, because all she wanted to do was rip his clothes off him.

How could she react so passionately to a man she'd only met the day before? she wondered uneasily. A man who was virtually a stranger. Probably because he didn't feel like one. Maybe it was because of all the research she'd done on him, but she felt as if she knew him in a way she'd never known another human being.

Role immersion, she thought to herself, mocking her reaction as she crossed the lobby under his intense gaze.

Why hadn't she invited him up to her apartment? Richard wondered. Her explanation about it not being safe to let strange men know where she lived was hardly valid because he wasn't. His gaze lingered on the enticing jiggle of her breasts as she walked toward him. Frustrated, yes, but strange, no. So why wouldn't she let him into her apartment? Could there be something in there that she didn't want him to see? Something connected with Moore and the embezzlement?

But what? Even the most inept embezzler wouldn't leave evidence lying around the living room.

Maggie threw a conversational gambit at him as she emerged onto the street. "What are we going to see?"

"It's Sondheim's latest. If you've already seen it, I can see if I can get tickets to something else."

"No, I haven't," Maggie said. "I mostly like his stuff."

Richard raised his arm and hailed a cruising taxi. Opening the door, he waited politely for Maggie to scoot inside first and felt his whole body clench with a violent twist of desire when her shawl slipped and he got a close look at the nonexistent back of her top. He could see the long, elegant line of her spine and the eminently touchable skin of her shoulders gleaming in the waning sunlight.

Damn, he thought in frustration. That top had to have been expressly designed to drive the average male into paroxysms of lust. And it was working. All he wanted to do was rip it off and make love to her. He wouldn't even have to rip it off, he thought as he got into the cab beside her. He could simply shove it to one side and then her breasts would be free. And then he could . . . He could stop behaving like a teenager at the mercy of his hormones, he told himself, jerking his imagination up short.

"How was your day?"

"I went to the office to take a look at things."

"Not much to see on a Saturday."

"At the moment, I'm more interested in the overall picture," he said.

"You have to like the overall picture or you wouldn't have bought the company."

"The company's future is very promising," Richard said. "Some of the banking programs the company has copyrighted are very innovative. There's an international potential that hasn't been tapped."

"Yes," Maggie said slowly, weighing his words. She already knew that some of the programs were innovative because she'd helped develop them. But if Richard really intended to sell those programs on the international market, then why had he gotten rid of the company's best salesman? Sam Moore was the kind of man who could sell anything to anyone and make him feel Sam was doing him a favor by letting him buy. It didn't add up.

"You don't like the idea of expanding?"

"I really don't care much one way or another," she said with absolute truth. Once she'd gotten revenge for Sam, she was gone. She had enough contacts in the field that she could have a job tomorrow simply by making a few phone calls.

Richard was taken aback by her response. He would've expected her to have been extremely interested in the tidbit of information he'd just fed her. She was a very ambitious woman. Her whole file was a testament to someone who had worked very hard and reaped the rewards of her work. She'd come a long way from the computer programmer she'd been hired as seven years ago.

But had she advanced on merit or on the strength of her relationship with the president of the company? If she had been personally involved with Moore, then everyone would have known about it in a company the size of Computer Solutions. That could be why her immediate supervisor had given her such glowing reviews. But how could he find out? He couldn't ask someone in the office because that might damage her reputation, and he didn't want to do that. He'd simply have to wait and see what happened.

The taxi pulled up in front of the theater and Maggie climbed out of the cab. She adjusted her shawl to cover her bare back while Richard paid the driver.

Putting his hand on the small of her back, he urged her toward the doors. Maggie shivered as the heat from his large hand seemed to burn through the thick silk of her shawl, searing her skin and warming her blood. She swallowed and kept her gaze firmly fixed on the polished brass doors in front of her as she tried to ignore the reaction churning through her. Sex, she told it. That's all it was.

It seemed unbelievable to her that she could have spent twenty-eight years virtually immune to sexual desire and then suddenly fall victim to it with the most inappropriate man. A man she would never have even considered dating under normal circumstances. He was too wealthy and far too sure of himself. Too much like her father.

She winced at the comparison. Nothing

will happen to you, she assured herself. Your mother only ran into trouble because she was an impressionable teenager who believed that love conquered all. And she couldn't have been too bright, either, Maggie thought tartly, if she had really believed that a wealthy, sophisticated man of forty was going to leave his equally wealthy, equally sophisticated wife to marry his mistress just because she was pregnant.

Had her mother gotten pregnant with her to try to force her lover to divorce his wife? Maggie suddenly wondered. Did she owe her very existence to her mother's attempt at moral blackmail? If so, her mother had chosen very unwisely because in order for that to work, the person being blackmailed had to have at least a few morals to begin with, and her father hadn't.

She shivered as she remembered the one and only time she'd seen him. She'd been thirteen, her mother had just died of an overdose and her whole world had collapsed. Their landlord had told her that he had called social services and that they would be by later that day to take her away. Fear and desperation had driven her down to her father's office to beg him to let her live with him.

She'd never forget the look of revulsion on his face. He had picked up the framed picture sitting on his desk and shoved it at her. It had been a studio portrait of a very pretty blond girl about her age. That was his daughter, he'd told her. His *only* daughter. He'd told her to get out. That there was no proof that Maggie was his daughter and that he'd make her sorry she was ever born if she tried to claim she was.

Maggie hadn't needed the threat. She had far too much pride to ever try to approach him again.

"What's wrong?" Richard asked. For a brief moment, she had looked so alone, so tormented that he'd wanted to gather her close and tell her not to worry because he'd protect her.

"Nothing." Maggie determinedly squashed her unhappy memories. "I was a million miles away."

Richard frowned slightly, not believing her, but unwilling to push and risk upsetting her more.

Pulling their tickets out of his inside jacket pocket, he showed them to the usher as they entered the auditorium. He checked the numbers on their tickets and made his way down the center aisle toward the front.

Maggie slipped past a woman wearing a pair of jeans and a glittery green top and sidestepped another in a lovely fuchsia silk dress before she finally reached their seats. She sat down, breathing an inward sigh of relief. She wasn't overdressed or under-dressed. Her outfit was within the norm.

"These are great seats," Maggie said and then immediately realized she shouldn't have made the comment. The women he dated would take good seats for granted. They would consider them their due.

"A cancellation, the lady at the ticket office told me," he said.

So he'd picked the tickets up in person, Maggie thought. Why hadn't he sent his PA to get them? From what she'd seen of Romanos in the office this past week, she'd bet he could get front-row tickets to the Second Coming.

"What ever happened to Romanos?" she asked, curious to know his whereabouts.

"He's meeting someone who's flying in from Washington this evening."

The auditorium's lights suddenly dimmed and the curtains opened, cutting off their conversation, to Maggie's relief. Her relief didn't last long when Richard picked up her hand and held it. Maggie shivered at the sensations that tore through her. Concentrating on what she was seeing and not on what she was feeling suddenly became a real challenge.

Chapter Six

"What did you think of the play?" Richard asked as they left the theater."

Maggie gnawed on the underside of her bottom lip as she tried to decide what to say. Should she rave about the performance because he had taken her, or should she be honest and give him her real opinion?

She stole a quick look at him, her gaze momentarily entangled in his gray eyes. He had the most fantastic eyes, she thought irrelevantly. Soft and velvety like pansies' petals but the color of the summer sky just before dawn. There were even minute specks of light glimmering in them like the fading stars.

Someone bumped her from behind in their haste to escape the theater, jarring her out of her thoughts. She had to keep focused, she told herself. Getting the better of Richard would be a hard enough task, but it would become impossible if she couldn't keep her mind on the job.

Partial honesty would probably be best, she finally decided.

"The songs were catchy, and the sets were great," she said praising the parts of the play she had liked.

"True, but I found the characters problematic," he said.

"In what way?"

"Every single one of them was exactly the same at the end of the play as at the beginning. They showed absolutely no personal growth. They didn't learn anything from their experiences."

To her surprise, he had picked up on the one thing that had bothered her.

"Maybe the author's point was that they were locked in their characters flaws," Maggie said, trying to be fair.

"But that's not realistic. In real life, people change," Richard insisted.

"Not from what I've seen. They just keep making variations on the same old mistakes."

Maggie ignored the flash of anger she felt as she remembered her father. *He* had certainly never changed. If anything, he'd hated her more on the day he died than he had on the day he found out about her existence.

"That might be true for a few, but I think most people are capable of adapting to changing conditions," Richard insisted.

"Being capable of change and being willing to put forth the effort to actually do it are two entirely different things," Maggie said. "When you get right down to it, the vast majority hate change. If they didn't, no one would smoke nor would anyone be overweight."

"You're oversimplifying," Richard said.

"No, I'm not. I'm . . ."

She suddenly broke off as she realized that she was no longer discussing the play; she was arguing about it. And that wasn't a smart thing to do. Letting him know she had views of her own was one thing. It was quite another to make him think that those views were in direct conflict with his own.

"You could be right," she reflected, forcing a conciliatory tone into her voice, even though she would have much preferred to continue the debate. "And when you get right down to it, it's only a play meant to entertain, not enlighten."

"If you say so," Richard said slowly, wondering why she was backpedaling so fast. And, more interesting, why had she felt so strongly about the subject in the first place? He'd bet a substantial sum that she'd been referring to something specific when she claimed that people don't change. Something painfully specific.

Could she have been thinking about Moore? Could they have had something going on the side? Could he have promised to divorce his wife and then changed his mind? Or had she been thinking of something else entirely?

He didn't know, and he wouldn't know if Maggie had been involved with Moore until his computer expert had tracked the flow of money. And even if she *had* been involved with Moore's embezzlement, that didn't automatically mean that there had been anything personal between them.

Frustration made him want to swear. And it wasn't just the mental frustration of not knowing exactly where she stood in all this mess.

"Do you like Italian?" Richard asked, changing the subject.

"I like anything I don't have to cook."

"Good, because I made reservations at an Italian restaurant." Richard hailed a passing taxi and bundled her into it. He gave the address of the restaurant that Daniel had recommended to the driver.

The taxi disgorged them fifteen minutes later in front of the crowded restaurant.

Maggie looked around. "Popular place," she observed as they made their way into the crowded foyer.

"That's what Daniel said. He had dinner here on one of his advance trips when we were negotiating to buy the company."

"You certainly kept the whole thing quiet."

"That's what the owner's lawyers wanted. Not that they weren't right. Most of our customers are banks and investment houses. They tend to recoil at the slightest hint of change."

"I'll say," Maggie muttered. "I wear a skirt whenever I have a meeting scheduled with one of them. Some of the older bankers tend to view women in pants as something vaguely obscene."

Richard's eyes lingered on the long length of her slim legs peering out from beneath the flirty hem of her clingy, black skirt. "I hate to be the one to break this bit of sexist news to you, but I think their desire to see you in a skirt has nothing to do with tradition and everything to do with liking to look at your gorgeous legs."

Maggie shot him a surprised look at his compliment, and a faint flush warmed her cheeks at the undisguised admiration she could see in his eyes. Her breathing shortened as a shaft of raw desire lanced through her. She was only excited because his admiring her body meant that she was that much closer to reaching her goal, she assured herself.

"I have reservations for two," Richard said to the harried-looking young hostess who was standing behind a cherry podium. "The name is Worthington."

The young woman looked up and her eyes widened as she got a good look at Richard. Covertly, her gaze swept over his tall, muscular body before lingering on his cleanly chiseled features.

"I made them this afternoon. I spoke to Cindy," Richard added when the woman simply continued to stare at him.

"Oh, yes!" she blurted out. "I'm Cindy. I remember your voice. It's so . . ." She broke off and a flush scorched over her face.

Maggie watched, torn between annoyance at the woman's unprofessional manner and sympathy because she was so clearly flustered by his overwhelming masculinity. Obviously, Richard was a lot more male than Cindy was used to dealing with.

"I remember you called right after I got here." Cindy checked the reservation book. "The regular hostess is off sick and my dad, who's the chef, called and asked me to help out. I'm a student nurse and I . . ." Her voice trailed away.

"Is something the matter?" Richard asked as an expression of horror chased over Cindy's face.

"I, um . . ." Cindy hurriedly ran her finger over the sheet of paper in front of her. "I . . ." She glanced furtively over her shoulder into the crowded restaurant and then blurted out, "I'm so sorry, but I forgot to write it down. I mean, I remember taking your reservation, but then that shipment of produce arrived and I had to unlock the back door and then . . ." Cindy caught her lower lip between her teeth, looking as if she was going to burst into tears.

Maggie tensed, waiting for Richard to explode. The program had been very specific — he didn't suffer fools gladly or any other way, for that matter. Nor did he have any patience whatsoever for incompetence and, no doubt about it, Cindy was hardly competent to handle the job that family loyalty had landed her with.

To Maggie's surprise, Richard simply glanced around Cindy at the jammed tables in the restaurant and then behind him at the people waiting in line to be seated before he said, "And you'll have no free tables for the next several hours?"

"I'm so sorry," Cindy whispered.

"It's hardly the end of the world," Richard said calmly. "We'll try your food another day."

"You aren't mad?" Cindy asked as if unable to believe he was taking it all so calmly.

"Of course not," he said. With a smile at Cindy, he took Maggie's arm and urged her toward the door.

Maggie went, uneasy at his reaction. Not that she wasn't grateful. She hated scenes and, if he'd demanded to see the manager, it could have been embarrassing. But the fact that he wasn't reacting as the program said he would worried her because if her program made one mistake it could make a second one. And she might not realize it until it was too late to correct it.

Richard could hardly suppress his glee. This was perfect. Instead of spending the evening in a crowded restaurant, he now had the perfect excuse to spend the rest of the evening alone with her. And it wouldn't even look suspicious.

"Nice girl but incompetent," Maggie offered, hoping he'd explain his reaction.

"Inexperienced, but it amounts to the same thing in the end. It's a shame, though, because I didn't get to eat lunch and I'm starved."

Maggie mentally ran through the contents of her refrigerator and rejected the idea of inviting him back to her place for a quick meal. She couldn't provide a meal for a mouse.

"Maybe we could try to find someplace else?" she suggested, loath to let the evening end prematurely.

"It's not likely without reservations. Not on a Saturday night. How about if we pick up something at a deli and take it back to your apartment?"

"Okay. There's a good deli a block and a half from me. We can have the taxi drop us off there and walk back."

"In those?" he said dubiously.

"They aren't uncomfortable," Maggie lied. She had no intention of letting him know that she normally wore flat shoes. She was going to pull off this sophisticated-woman-of-the-world disguise if it killed her. Or her feet — whichever came first.

Maggie spent the entire taxi ride and the quick stop at the deli debating the wisdom of what she was doing. She couldn't decide if inviting him back to her apartment was a natural progression in her campaign to get him to fall for her or if she was making a major miscalculation.

Richard Worthington was a man in every sense of the word. He not only wasn't into sexual self-denial, he probably wouldn't even recognize the concept. Would he expect the evening to end by making love to her?

A sudden burst of heat exploded deep in her abdomen and she felt lightheaded. She firmly faced the fact that it wasn't revulsion she was feeling. For the first time in her adult life, she craved physical contact with a man, and yet Richard was the one man she couldn't have. Going to bed with him would be a disaster, both to her plans for revenge and her future.

Surreptitiously, she studied him as they left the deli and started down the street toward her apartment. Her gaze lingered on the breadth of his shoulders before moving down his arm to linger on his long fingers, which were holding their carrier bag of food.

What would it feel like to have those fingers touch her? To have them slip over her skin? A prickle of awareness skated over her skin, raising goosebumps as it went. The very idea made her feel restless and edgy and totally unlike her normal, calm self, and she didn't like the sensation. Being out of control was dangerous. Especially around a man like Richard. He belonged to a class that took. A class that viewed women like her as little more than conveniences to be enjoyed and then disposed of. She absolutely couldn't allow herself to forget that.

Richard stepped aside while she unlocked the lobby door. "Here we are." Maggie pushed open the door to her apartment and hastily looked around. To her relief, she hadn't left anything lying around. Not that she was in the habit of being messy. Her apartment's small size made neatness imperative.

Intensely curious about her, Richard looked around. The room was claustrophobically small — standard New York City-size — but cozy. The colors were soothing pastels in shades of green and blue, and the furniture was minimal — just a loveseat, chair and a desk with a large computer on it against one wall.

Handing the carrier of food to Maggie, he walked over to the large painting that dominated one wall, studied it for a moment and then said, "Botticelli, *A Florentine Lady*."

Maggie blinked in surprise. According to her program, his taste in paintings ran to the French Impressionists. And yet he'd not only recognized the artist — something no other visitor had done — but also known the name of the painting.

Richard Worthington was turning out to be very smart. The worrisome question was, was he as perceptive as he was intelligent? It didn't matter, she told herself. She had buried her real motivation deep enough that he would never find it. Not only that but he had no reason to even go looking.

"I've always thought Botticelli's paintings were restful. I saw the original last year at the Louvre and bought a copy to bring home."

"Yes, I like him, too. I've got one of his religious paintings in my study at home and I like to simply immerse myself in the colors."

Great, Maggie thought grimly. *I go to the Louvre to look at Botticelli; he goes to his study.*

Brushing aside the reminder of just how unequal their positions were as irrelevant, she headed toward her minuscule kitchen. "Follow me. We can fill our plates in the kitchen," she said.

Maggie realized her mistake immediately. She should have brought plates and silverware out to the living room. The kitchen was so small they were practically touching.

Reaching into the overhead cabinet, she pulled down two dinner plates and handed one to him, trying to ignore the warmth from his large body that seemed to be crowding her against the countertop.

She took a deep breath in an attempt to steady her racing heart, but it didn't work. Instead, her action pulled the scent of his cologne straight into her lungs. The faintly lemony aroma scraped across her nerves, sparking them to vibrant life. She wanted to inch closer to him, to press her nose against the tantalizing strip of skin showing between his ink-black hair and the whiteness of his shirt collar and breathe deeply of the man himself. She wanted to run her lips along his jaw and explore the texture of his emerging beard. She wanted . . .

". . . Napkin?"

The last word he'd said finally penetrated her absorption in his body and Maggie forcibly shook off the sexual web he seemed to so effortlessly spin around her.

Maybe there was more of her mother's self-destructive tendencies in her than she'd originally thought, she considered uneasily.

"Napkins," she repeated and then hastily opened a drawer to get some out. She handed him several.

"What would you like to drink?" she asked, wincing at the bright, hostessy tone in her voice. She sounded like a bad parody of Martha Stewart.

"Do you have any beer?"

Opening her refrigerator, she pulled out a bottle of Sam Adams dark ale that one of her girlfriends was fond of. "Is this okay?"

"Sure." He took the bottle and, filling his plate with food, started back into the living room.

"Do you want a glass for your beer?" she asked as she followed him.

Richard grinned at her, and her stomach clenched at the laughter glimmering in his eyes.

"You must not drink much beer," he said.

"Beer is an acquired taste I've never acquired."

"Not even during your college years? Most kids kick over the traces the first time they get away from home. I sure did."

"No, not even then," she said shortly. She'd been much too busy working two jobs and studying to indulge in parties. Other people might look back on their college years with fond remembrance, but all she remembered was years of not enough sleep, too much work and being perennially hungry.

Richard took a long swig of beer, inwardly frowning as he suddenly realized something. If she didn't like beer, then why was it in her refrigerator? Who had she bought it for? It couldn't have been for him. She hadn't even known him until yesterday. Did she have an ongoing relationship with some man who liked dark ale? His fingers clenched around the bottle in rejection of the idea of Maggie in another man's arms.

She'd denied being involved with anyone else, he told himself. And she'd hardly have gone out with him if she were presently involved with someone. Although she might if she was involved with Moore's embezzlement and she wanted to get close to him to find out what he knew, the unpalatable thought occurred to him.

No, he rejected that notion. He knew it couldn't be true because she'd accepted the first date with him before she'd known who he was. The thought soothed him.

Maggie looked up to find Richard staring at her, and her heart sank at the speculative expression she could see in his eyes. What was he thinking? she wondered uneasily. Was he comparing her unfavorably to the women he normally dated? According to her research, they tended to be successful, self-sufficient types. And in order to compare favorably, she needed to radiate self-confidence. She swallowed uneasily. Not an easy task when the only place she truly felt self-confident was at work.

So how did one go about radiating self-confidence? she wondered. Flirt with him? Confident women flirted. But if she did, she might invite a whole lot more than she intended — or than she could handle.

"I think I'll get myself a soda," she retreated. "Can I get you something else?"

"I'm okay," Richard said.

He was a whole lot more than just okay, Maggie thought, her eyes focused on the firm line of his mouth as she moved around him. He was the most spectacular man she'd ever met, bar none. He . . .

Her mind was so caught up with cataloguing Richard's attractions that she totally forgot to pay attention to the fact that she was wearing very high heels. She tripped over his oversized feet and hastily jerked back, trying to regain her balance.

"Careful!" Richard reached out and

grabbed her wrist, tipping her into his lap.

Maggie fell awkwardly, her face pressed into the hard warmth of his shoulder. For a long moment, she didn't move. She simply absorbed the feel of his hard thighs beneath her hips and the pressure of his chest against her shoulder.

She took a deep breath, pulling the earthy scent of clean, warm male deep into her lungs. It was an exotic blend of aromas that was totally alien to her. Alien yet compulsively seductive.

Her eyelids felt too heavy to hold up and she instinctively started to snuggle closer, freezing when she felt the proof of his reaction against her hips. He wasn't unaffected by holding her in his lap, she thought with a sense of wonder. He felt something, too.

A sensation of power swept over her, and she tilted her head back against his shoulder, peering up into his face from beneath half-closed eyes. Dark-red scored his cheekbones, and his gray eyes glittered with the strength of his emotions. Fascinated, she watched as the tiny lights in his eyes came closer.

It wasn't until his mouth closed over hers with a rough urgency that she realized just how close they had come. A second later, she was incapable of rational thought. All she could do was react to the feel of his hard arms crushing her to him. To the feel of his warm lips pressing against hers. Her blood began to pound through her veins, beating in her ears and drowning out the voice of reason telling her she had to keep a mental distance.

It was as if Richard were suddenly supplying something vital to her body. Something that made all her senses sharper, more intense. Something that had always been lacking, and she hadn't even realized it.

Instinctively, she clutched his shoulders and tried to pull him closer to intensify the sensation. Her breathing fractured as she felt his tongue lightly outline her lips and she opened her mouth. His tongue slipped inside, erotically stroking, and Maggie moaned, at a loss to deal with the excitement cascading through her.

Oddly enough, it was the tormented sound of her own voice that sliced her free from the sensual web she was caught in. She jerked back and scrambled off his lap, appalled at how mindless she'd been in his arms. Her plans had been the furthest thing from her mind. In his arms, she had momentarily become someone she didn't even know, and it scared her. She didn't want to lose control. Losing control would leave her vulnerable. And to be vulnerable to someone as ruthless as Richard Worthington . . .

She couldn't make that mistake.

Chapter Seven

"I was beginning to think you wouldn't make it in today, Richard." Daniel Romanos greeted him Monday as he entered the opulent lobby of the building where the company's offices were housed.

"Daniel." Richard automatically glanced behind the man, looking for Maggie, even though he knew the chances of running into her in the lobby at one o'clock in the afternoon were very small. But even so, he still found himself keeping an eye out for her. The kiss they'd shared on Saturday night had left him both uncomfortably aware of her and longing for more. Much more.

When a problem with one of his French subsidiaries had mushroomed into a potential disaster early Sunday morning, it had taken all his willpower not to drop the problem in Daniel's hands and call Maggie instead. The very strength of the desire he'd felt to do just that was what had stopped him. He intended for her to be his companion for the six weeks he'd be in

New York, but he refused to allow her to interfere with what was really important: his work.

"Did you clear up the problem in France?" Daniel asked.

"Yes, it's taken care of. For the time being, at least. I'm beginning to think that Faberge isn't up to running things over there. Keep an eye on his performance, would you?"

"Sure, I'll make a note of it. I thought I'd give you a quick rundown on the situation here on the way up to the office," Daniel told him as they entered the empty elevator.

"Does that computer expert have anything to report yet?"

"All I know for a fact is that he's been here since Saturday afternoon. I sent for him when you called to say you were on your way in. He's waiting for you in your office."

"So what's the mood in the place this morning?" Richard asked.

"Sullen with homicidal overtones," Daniel said grimly. "If I were you, Richard, I'd think twice about drinking any coffee that Emily Adams, Moore's previous secretary, gives you."

"Hmm." Richard remembered Maggie's

comment about how the secretary had hated him so much she wouldn't even deliver a package to his apartment.

"Once they realize that I have no intention of closing down the firm, things will settle down."

Daniel grimaced. "I don't think it's going to be that simple. From what I can gather, the crux of their dislike is the fact that you fired Moore. Apparently, he was very popular with everyone from the janitor to the vice president."

"Maybe he was popular because he was sharing the millions he embezzled!"

Daniel shrugged. "Maybe, and maybe he was just one of those charismatic guys that everyone liked. From everything I've seen, he was one helluva salesman, and great salesmen are usually likable guys."

Maggie had certainly liked Moore, Richard remembered uneasily.

"Of course, if I were to discreetly leak what he did . . ." Daniel suggested.

"Forget it." Richard shoved his long fingers through his thick hair. "One of the conditions when we bought the company from his mother-in-law was that we'd keep our mouths shut about both Moore's embezzlement and his gambling."

"Why'd she tell you in the first place if

she was trying to keep her son-in-law's indiscretions a secret?" Daniel asked.

"She didn't have a choice. It would have come out when we audited the books. By that point, I don't think she cared all that much about protecting him. I think the ones she wanted to shield from any unpleasant publicity were her daughter and grandkids."

"I could plant the information so that she would never be able to trace it back to you," Daniel suggested.

"No." Richard flatly vetoed the idea. "Do you think any of them would try to sabotage the company to get even?"

"It wouldn't be very logical. I mean it's their livelihood, too."

"Only for as long as they stay, and I'll bet anything that at least half the staff are actively looking for new jobs and the other half have feelers out," Richard said.

The elevator doors suddenly opened into a spacious lobby area and Daniel lead the way across what seemed like acres of gray carpeting.

Daniel paused in front of a large mahogany desk. "Ms. Adams, this is Mr. Worthington."

Richard watched as the woman's face froze into a blank mask and her plump figure tensed. Even her short, graying hair seemed to bristle in rejection in their presence.

"Mr. Worthington," she nodded abruptly. "A Mr. Zylinski is waiting for you in your office. He said you sent for him."

"Thank you." Richard ignored her frigid manner and treated her with his normal, professional courtesy.

"See what I mean?" Daniel muttered as he led the way into Richard's office. "One could get frostbite around that woman. My inclination is to transfer her out of this office and replace her with someone who is, at least, pleasant."

"But probably no more trustworthy. For now, simply ignore her manner. Maybe all she needs is a chance to come to terms with the fact that the old order changeth."

Daniel shot him a disbelieving glance. "You really think so?"

Richard grinned. "No. I think the lady hates our guts. I also think she'll leave as soon as she can. Let's give her some space to go. If she doesn't change her attitude or leave, then I'll have a talk with her."

"You're a braver man than I." Daniel pushed open the door to a large office with windows that looked down on the street twenty stories below.

Richard glanced around the opulent surroundings, taking in the antique mahogany desk and glass-fronted bookcases. In the corner was a brown leather sofa and a pair of chairs. Seated in one chair was a small, chubby man who bounced to his feet.

"Richard, this is Jeff Zylinski."

Richard shook the man's hand, tossed his briefcase onto the desk and cut to the heart of the matter. "What have you found out?"

Zylinski rubbed his pudgy hands together and said, "It was a very neat embezzlement scheme, particularly for a novice. With a little practice, your Mr. Moore could be dangerous."

"He cost his in-laws over two million dollars in the course of three years," Richard said dryly. "That's plenty dangerous. But what I'm really interested in is was anyone else involved in the scheme with him?"

"I can't answer that just yet. I'm still tracking the money. He bounced it around quite a bit before he made it disappear."

"I see." Richard clenched his teeth against his sense of raging impatience. He had to know if Maggie had been involved before he got in any deeper with her. "How long will it take you to have an answer for me?"

"I should have a preliminary report for you in a couple of days," Zylinski said.

"I hope I don't need to stress the need for discretion," Richard said. "As far as anyone other than Daniel and myself are concerned, this is a routine audit."

"Keeping my mouth shut goes without saying," Zylinski assured him. "Although I've always found that who tries to pump me for information can be interesting."

"Oh?" Richard eyed him levelly. "And I take it someone has tried to find out what you're doing?"

"Two someones. Ms. Iceberg in the outer office, and a gorgeous brunette over in the computer-development section named Maggie something or other." Zylinski's eyes gleamed. "If I were twenty years younger, I'd sure let her try to worm my secrets out of me."

Richard tensed at his unexpected words. "When did you run across Maggie?"

"This morning. She asked me who I was and what I was doing. The rest of the staff simply kept giving me sideways glances. She came right out with it. I like a direct woman."

"What did you tell her?" Richard asked.

Zylinski chuckled. "I started to give her double-talk, but she interrupted me and told me that if I couldn't or wouldn't tell her to just say so. Not to insult her intelligence with a lot of mumbo jumbo."

Zylinski shook his head in admiration. "Usually women go all flirtatious and try a con when they want to know something. That Maggie is a rare lady."

Maggie was certainly rare, Richard thought grimly. But the question was, A rare what? Could she be a thief? But would it even be theft? Mrs. Wright had eaten the losses and refused to press charges against her son-in-law, so legally, he wasn't sure if a crime had even been committed.

"Let me know the minute you find out anything," Richard told him. "Do you have my cell number?"

"I'll give it to him," Daniel said as he escorted Zylinski to the door.

Richard sank down into the oversized leather chair behind the desk and stared blankly at a picture of an English hunting scene on the wall over the sofa as he considered what Zylinski had said.

Maggie was a very intelligent woman, and she was direct. She didn't appear to play games. If she wanted to know something, she asked. So when a strange man showed up and started going through the company's computer files, she wouldn't think twice about challenging him. The explanation could be that simple. Or it could be much more ominous. There was no way to know at this stage, he thought in frustration. Asking her certainly wouldn't do any good. It would only alert her to the fact that she was under suspicion.

"Am I scheduled for anything this afternoon?" Richard asked, wondering how he could manage to see Maggie without being too obvious about it. Until everyone's emotions settled down and they realized that he wasn't some kind of monster out to make their lives miserable, it would be best if he didn't let people know he was interested in her. He didn't want her to be the target of anyone's spite.

A surge of protectiveness welled up in him. He didn't mind being treated like Typhoid Mary himself, but he didn't want to expose Maggie to the same treatment. Especially since he'd be gone in six weeks and she'd be stuck here.

Although, perhaps, once he'd cleared her of any involvement with Moore, he could transfer her to the San Francisco office, where he spent most of his time. His original plan had been to send a team from San Francisco to New York to learn the banking programs from the people who had written them. But it would work equally well to send a team from New York to San Francisco and have them train his people there. And who better to head up the team than Maggie, who'd been involved in writing most of the programs.

Daniel checked his appointment book. "There's a meeting set up with the director of development from Second Citizen's Bank and Trust. They're buying an accounting program from us. The only hang-up appears to be the modifications they want. Moore was directly involved in the early talks they had with us, so I think you ought to put in an appearance, otherwise they might feel slighted."

Richard grimaced. "And God forbid that the customer should have his tender feelings slighted. Who else is going to be at this meeting?"

"Just a Ms. Romer from development who has been working on the modifications the bank wants, and I presume a secretary to take notes. They seem to be very casual in their approach to things here," Daniel said in disapproval.

"They're a midsize company that never mentally overcame thinking of themselves as a small one. We'll change that, but not right this minute. When is the meeting?"

"Two."

Richard checked the time on his thin, gold Rolex. "Less than an hour. Remind me a few minutes beforehand. In the meantime, I want to check in with Hammet back in San Francisco about the deal he's putting together for the Chinese."

"Will do," Daniel said as Richard reached for the phone.

"He's here!" Kate burst into Maggie's office.

Maggie looked up from the spreadsheet she was studying and stared blankly at the young woman.

"He who?"

"The new owner, and is he hot! I caught a glimpse of him when he got off the elevator. I mean the guy is totally buff. I'd love to see him stripped." Kate shivered theatrically.

Maggie froze as the memory of Richard's bare chest filled her mind. A heated warmth began to gather deep in her stomach, and a sense of longing shortened her breath. Kate wasn't the only one who'd love to get him out of his clothes, Maggie thought ruefully.

After that kiss Saturday night, all she'd

been able to think about on Sunday was sex. Hers. His. The two of them together. Suddenly, a subject that had never been of much interest to her in the past became quite consuming.

"Maggie, would you quit thinking about work and start thinking about something interesting for a change. I had hoped you were going to start acting like a normal woman when you started wearing clothes that fit, but let me tell you, sister, it takes more than just a new wardrobe to appeal to men."

"Not at work, it doesn't," Maggie said, having no intention of telling Kate what had really caused her abstract expression. "And work beckons. I have a meeting in ten minutes with a bunch of bankers."

Maggie got to her feet and picked up the stack of printouts sitting on the edge of her desk.

"Ah, that would explain the sexy power suit." Kate nodded sagely. "I really like it. All you need is a red carnation for your lapel and you could pass as a gangster's moll."

"You think?" Maggie stared down uncertainly at the black, double-breasted, pin-striped suit with its straight skirt that ended just above her knee. She'd bought this suit hoping it was an acceptable compromise between something fashionable that would appeal to Richard and something conservative that wouldn't offend the bankers' chauvinistic attitudes. But if Kate thought this outfit was sexy, maybe she'd made a mistake. Unfortunately, if she had, it was too late to change. An image of Richard's dark features floated through her mind. It was too late to change a lot of things.

"That was a compliment," Kate hurriedly told her. "Even a banker has to appreciate you in that suit."

"As long as they appreciate my program, I don't care what they think of me personally. I'll see you later." Maggie headed toward the door.

"If Worthington is at your meeting, try to get him to come back here so I can view him up close and personal," Kate begged her.

Maggie nodded and left the room, hoping the excitement she felt wasn't visible in her face. She doubted that Richard would be there. He'd probably be too busy taking over the reins of the company. But even the possibility that she might catch a glimpse of him in the office made her day brighter.

Maggie got in the empty elevator and pushed the button for the twenty-second floor, where the conference rooms were located. Thirty seconds later, the elevator doors opened with a refined *ping,* and Maggie hurried toward the meeting room, hoping her clients weren't early. She needed a strong shot of caffeine before she could deal with them.

Maggie pushed open the conference-room door and stepped inside.

Time seemed to slow as she saw Richard's large body seated at the far end of the conference table. The sunlight coming in through the plate-glass window behind him bathed him in a brilliant light that seemed to emphasize his size.

Greedily, her eyes traced over the breadth of his shoulders. He might be a businessman, but he really was built more like the plumber he'd pretended to be. *Not even his perfectly tailored Armani suit could disguise his hard-packed muscles.*

She stole a quick glance at his face and a flush scorched her cheeks as she found his eyes focused on her mouth. Instinctively, she ran the tip of her tongue over her bottom lip, caught off guard by the hunger that suddenly flared in the depth of his gray eyes.

For a moment, her heart seemed to stop, and then it began to race. She wanted to fling herself into his arms and kiss him again. And keep kissing him until she was as good at kissing as he was. And once she'd mastered kissing, she'd like to move on to . . .

"Good morning, Maggie." Richard's deep voice flowed over her agitated nerve endings, making her feel as if she were standing on the edge of a precipice and one unwary move would send her plunging into unknown depths.

"Hi." Maggie tried for a casual, throwaway tone, but from the way his eyebrows shot up, she didn't think she'd been successful. Stalling to give herself time to regain her composure, Maggie began to take her notes out of her leather folder.

Once she had them arranged in front of her, she walked over to the coffeepot and poured herself a cup.

"Are you going to stay for the meeting?" she asked, trying to sound no more than nominally interested.

"Yes," Richard said. "From the preliminary report I read, this project could have applications far beyond banking."

"True." Maggie relaxed slightly when he made no attempt to move the conversation into the personal realm. Work she could handle. Work she knew inside out. It was only her emotions that tied her up in knots.

"Who told you about the ramifications of this program?" she asked curiously as she returned to her seat. "Daniel Romanos or that tubby little man who was rifling through our computer files all weekend?"

Richard's eyes narrowed slightly. "What makes you think he was here all weekend?" he probed.

"I didn't say he was *here* all weekend. I said he was in our files all weekend. With the proper codes, he could have accessed them from anywhere."

"I'm still curious as to why you think he was working on the files all weekend."

Maggie studied him for a long moment, trying to figure out the odd note in his voice. She couldn't. Not for the first time, she cursed her lack of experience with men. She had no idea how their thought processes worked. Particularly not one as sophisticated as Richard Worthington. But she had the odd feeling that there wasn't a man alive who could have prepared her for Richard. He was definitely one-of-a-kind. He had to be experienced to be believed.

"When I logged on this morning, I discovered that he'd been through my files as well as a lot of other ones, so I asked him what he was doing and on whose authority he was doing it. Some of our programs contain highly classified information. Not only that, but some you could use to get into our client banks' files and the mind boggles at what one could do if one had a larcenous mind."

"You think Zylinski has? He looks like a latter-day Santa Claus."

And looks could be deceptive, Maggie thought with a shudder as she remembered her biological father, who had looked like the quintessential country gentleman and had acted like a cold, unfeeling bastard. "Looks don't mean a thing," she said flatly.

Richard wondered what was responsible for her bleak expression. Certainly not Zylinski's physical appearance. Could she be afraid of what he might uncover?

Richard leaned back in his chair and allowed his eyes to wander over the way her parody of a man's suit fit snuggly over her exquisitely shaped breasts. He wanted to slowly undo the three buttons that held the jacket together and peel it back to reveal what was underneath. Was she wearing anything? His body clenched at the thought.

If he didn't get her into bed soon, his concentration was going to be shot. He couldn't remember ever wanting a woman as badly as he wanted Maggie, and yet he couldn't pinpoint why. Granted, she was attractive, but no more so than the women he normally dated. No, there was more to her compulsive appeal than her physical appearance. It was as if, on some unconscious level, both his mind and his body recognized her. And that was ridiculous. He was not — and never had been — a romantic. He was pragmatic about everything, and that included his sex life. He didn't have love affairs; he had affairs — period. He never lied or pretended to feel more than he did. He was totally upfront about what he wanted from a woman and what he was willing to give in exchange. If the woman in question couldn't handle that, then he moved on.

So what was it about Maggie that made him hesitant to be too blunt? To do anything that might scare her off? He didn't have a clue.

"Oh, I wouldn't say that. You, for example, look gorgeous in that outfit."

To his surprise, a flush stained her cheeks and, for a second, she seemed to shrink in on herself. But why? he wondered. Why would a simple compliment embarrass her? Looking like she did, she should get compliments on a daily basis. So why didn't she parry them like most of the women he knew? There was something about this whole situation he was missing, and it worried him. Loose ends had a nasty way of suddenly tripping up the unwary.

"So do you," Maggie finally said, hoping that if she disconcerted him, he'd stop the compliments, which she didn't feel comfortable fielding. "But that doesn't mean anything except that you were blessed at birth with a combination of genes that our society finds aesthetically pleasing. And that you can afford to enhance your natural appearance with Armani suits and ties."

Richard blinked, totally taken aback by her comment. He couldn't decide if he'd been complimented or not. All he knew for certain was that she was not reacting like any other woman he'd ever met. Usually, women fawned over him, hanging on his every word.

"Helmut Lang." He focused on one thing he did understand.

"What?" Maggie looked confused.

"My tie. It's Helmut Lang, not Armani."

"Oh," Maggie murmured. Her program

hadn't mentioned that he bought from Helmut Lang. That was the second thing it had missed. Both things had been relatively minor, but they were starting to add up, she thought uneasily.

"But you still didn't tell me why Zylinski was checking the computer files," she said, returning to the original subject with her usual tenacity.

So much for distracting her. Richard felt an odd combination of annoyance at her persistence and admiration that she refused to be sidetracked.

"He's checking the flow of money in the company over the past three years." Richard decided to give her part of the truth and see what she did with it.

Maggie wrinkled her small nose. "If you don't want to tell me what he's doing, it's your business. Just say so, but please don't lie to me."

Richard blinked, taken aback by her reaction.

"Why would I be lying to you?"

"How would I know? I'd probably have to know what he's looking for in our files to figure that out. And I'm perfectly willing to admit that I have no need to know."

"Why won't you accept my explanation?"

"Because I'm a businesswoman. And anyone with even a hint of experience will tell you that you examine the financial records of a company *before* you buy, not after. There's no point after. And the enthusiasm with which that guy was going through the files would hint at a very big point."

"Maybe he's simply a man who throws himself into his work?"

Maggie grimaced. "Could be. He obviously throws himself into his dinner."

Richard's lips twitched at her disgruntled expression. If the bankers weren't due here any second, he'd have been tempted to take her in his arms and kiss her ill humor away.

The sound of the door opening made him glad he'd exercised restraint. He turned as Daniel escorted the bank's three representatives into the conference room and then watched as Maggie greeted them with the perfect blend of competence and deference.

Richard gritted his teeth in sudden annoyance as the youngest of the three men stared at the way her suit molded to her breasts. What the hell was the matter with him? Richard thought in annoyance. Maggie was selling a computer program, not herself, and the jerk had no reason to eye her as if she were on offer.

The young man turned to him as Daniel introduced Richard, recoiling slightly at the anger that Richard made no attempt to hide. A faint flush washed over the man's cheeks, and he hastily sank into a chair with only a cursory nod at Richard.

Satisfied that the man had gotten the message, Richard shook hands with the bank's two senior vice presidents and sat down to listen as Maggie took charge of the meeting.

As the presentation unfolded, he felt rather like a proud parent whose child had just distinguished herself. She was clear, concise and thorough. There was no ambiguity about what she proposed to do for the bank. The only downside was that the information was delivered in a husky voice that made Richard think of warm sheets, steamy nights and sex — especially sex.

Taking a deep breath, Richard tried to pay closer attention to what she was saying and not how she was saying it. It was hard. He didn't want to work around Maggie. He wanted to play. He very badly wanted to play, and he couldn't until Zylinski had cleared her of being mixed up in Moore's embezzlement scheme.

But one thing was now crystal clear, Richard thought as he listened to her respond to the bankers' questions. Maggie hadn't owed her job to Moore's favoritism. She held it because she was very knowledgeable about what she did. Not only knowledgeable, but she possessed that rare ability to translate technical programs into layman's English that the customer could understand. She clearly earned her salary.

In fact, she could undoubtedly make more at another place. Much more. So why hadn't she gone somewhere else? Unless she was making something on the side with Moore? He shifted restlessly, not liking the direction of his thoughts.

He'd find out the truth soon enough. Until then, he needed to keep his mind *off* getting Maggie Romer in bed!

Chapter Eight

Maggie let herself into her apartment and dropped her briefcase on the floor just inside the door. Kicking off her shoes, she sank into the couch and wiggled her aching toes. Her feet were never going to survive her plans for revenge. She just hoped that whatever sadist had come up with the idea of pointed toes and stiletto heels as the height of fashion had to spend a couple of hundred years in purgatory wearing them in a size too small.

She sighed despondently. The worst part was that it was beginning to look as if it was all going to be for nothing. Richard hadn't called her since Saturday night and this was Thursday. She hadn't even talked to him at work since that meeting with the bankers on Monday.

Unhappily, Maggie caught her lower lip between her teeth. Somehow, she'd managed to turn him off, and she didn't know how. She'd been over and over her program, trying to figure out what had gone wrong, and she still didn't have a clue.

Unless . . . unless he'd never been all that turned on in the first place? Maybe he'd simply been at loose ends last weekend and she'd been vaguely acceptable and available. Or maybe her lack of skill at kissing had made him realize that she wasn't as sophisticated as the women he normally dated and that had made him back off. Maybe he'd been worried that she would read more than he'd intended into their two dates? He'd certainly made a point of not being into permanent relationships.

A feeling of loss swept over her, but only because it looked like she was going to have to give up on her plans for revenge, she told herself. She didn't care on her own behalf. She . . .

Maggie jumped as the phone suddenly rang.

For a second, she considered letting the machine pick up, but she finally decided to answer it. She needed a distraction, even if it was only someone trying to sell her something.

"Hello?" she said, and her fingers suddenly tightened around the receiver as the husky timbre of Richard's deep voice poured through her mind.

"Did I catch you at a bad time?"

"No." She tried for a bright, confident tone. "I just got in from work," she added, hoping he'd assume the breathless sound of her voice was caused by rushing and not by the relief she felt at hearing from him.

"At six-thirty?"

"Hmm. One of our clients called at three and said that the program we sold them wasn't working. Customer service couldn't figure out what was going on, so they called me since I helped write it."

"Were you able to fix it?" Richard asked more because he wanted to hear her talk than because he really cared about a design problem. He leaned back in his chair and let the sexy sound of her voice soak into his mind, revitalizing him.

His original plan had been to wait until Zylinski was able to tell him what — if anything — her involvement with Moore had been, but Zylinski had come down with the flu on Tuesday and was still out. And Richard couldn't wait one second longer to be with Maggie. His frustration level at being deprived of her company had steadily risen all week long until it had reached critical mass this afternoon. He'd finally decided that there was no harm in dating Maggie as long as he didn't go to bed with her until Zylinski cleared her.

That way, he could keep all of his options open.

"One does not fix rampant egotism!" she said, annoyance coloring her voice. "I finally discovered that their head computer person, who thinks he's God's gift to programming, decided to modify our original program. What he actually did was screw the whole thing up. It's going to take a couple of people working through the weekend to have it back on-line by Monday, when they need it to print some reports for their clients. But he won't try that again," she added with satisfaction. "I reminded their president that they merely lease the program. That if they make any modifications to it, they are in violation of their contract."

"You aren't one of the people fixing it, are you?" Richard demanded, seeing his embryonic plans for the weekend disappearing.

"No, now that the problem has been identified, any good programmer can do it, and we have lots of good ones at the company. Sam put together a superb staff." Maggie put in a good word for him. To her frustration, Richard ignored it.

"Actually, I called you to ask a favor. I need to pick up a gift and I haven't a clue as to what to get her. I'll buy you dinner if you'll help me pick something out."

Maggie bit her lip as jealousy exploded in her mind, catching her by surprise. Who was this *her* Richard was buying a gift for, and what was the occasion he was celebrating? According to both her research and what he'd told her, he wasn't involved with anyone at the moment. Apparently not even her. The thought depressed her.

Was his asking her to help him buy a gift for another woman a sophisticated way of telling her he wasn't interested in her personally? She had no idea, but no matter what his motivation, she wasn't going to turn down the chance to spend time with him. Not while there was the slightest possibility that she might be able to avenge Sam, she justified.

"Sure, I'll help. Where do you want to eat?" she asked, mentally wincing at the thought of shoving her feet back into those torturous heels again. Life had definitely been more comfortable when her wardrobe had been chosen as camouflage.

"Why don't we just walk around until we find a nice-looking restaurant, and we can go shopping after dinner," Richard said. "I'll pick you up in fifteen minutes. I'm starved. I managed to miss lunch again."

She was starved, too, but not for food.

Maggie faced the unpalatable fact squarely. Somehow, her plans for revenge were being swamped by her growing fascination with Richard, and she had no idea what to do about it. "Make it twenty," Maggie said. "I need to change."

"Twenty it is. See you then. Bye."

Maggie hung up the receiver and hurried into the bathroom to shower away all the frustrations of her long day.

Fifteen minutes later, she hurriedly buckled up a pair of strappy sandals that were almost comfortable to walk in and then pulled on the white fitted jacket that matched her pants. She paused a second to admire the way the crystal trim around the deeply scooped neckline of her cotton tank glittered. Twisting around, she checked the back view, noting the smooth line of her hips and thighs with satisfaction. She didn't feel anywhere near as exposed in this outfit as she had when she'd bought it four weeks ago. By the time Richard left for California, she'd be able to wear the outfit without a second thought.

Maggie swallowed at the sudden surge of panic she felt at the thought of Richard leaving. Of never seeing him again.

The sound of the buzzer from the street door distracted her and she determinedly banished her unhappy thoughts. Richard was here, and they were going to spend the evening together. The future could worry about itself.

She grabbed her white purse and rushed out of the apartment. She was halfway across the lobby when she saw him through the outside door and her breath caught in her throat. He was wearing a pair of cream cotton chinos, a pale blue T-shirt and a black linen jacket.

Maggie swallowed as her mouth suddenly watered. He looked gorgeous. Quintessentially masculine. And she wanted nothing so much as to grab him and kiss him. Grab him and do a whole lot more than merely kiss him . . .

She bit her lip as she made her way across the lobby. She just wished she knew what it was about Richard that affected her so strongly so she could inoculate herself against it. In order for her plan to work, she had to keep her distance emotionally, and she wasn't doing too good a job of it at the moment.

And her job wasn't made any easier by the fact that he almost seemed to have a split personality. When he was out with her, he was a fascinating, sexy man, and yet at work this week, he'd shown himself to be both impressively single-minded and compulsively hardworking.

Pushing open the lobby door, she stepped onto the sidewalk, watching as Richard turned and caught sight of her. Something flared momentarily in his gray eyes and she shivered in response. Suddenly, her skin felt too tight for her body and she found it hard to breathe.

Whatever else Richard Worthington was, he was no fool. A frisson of unease chased down her spine at the thought of his probable reaction if he ever found out about her plans for revenge. He wouldn't, she assured herself. No one but she knew, and she certainly wasn't going to tell him. She didn't have a suicidal bone in her body.

"What's wrong?" His eyes suddenly narrowed.

"Wrong?"

"For a moment there, you looked . . . fearful," he finally said, wondering if she was afraid of what Zylinski might uncover. If she really had been involved with Moore, then this past week must have been an intolerable strain on her.

"Just tired," Maggie lied. "I'll be fine after dinner."

"Okay." Richard let the subject drop. "I thought I'd have the cab drop us off by

Rockefeller Center. We can find someplace to eat near there."

Maggie followed him over to the waiting car.

A nerve twitched beside Richard's mouth as she climbed in and the material of her slacks stretched over her perfectly shaped hips. His palm tingled with the urge to stroke them and then continue upward to explore that tantalizing strip of skin he could see between the top of her slacks and the bottom of that stretchy top.

He clenched his hand to dispel his compulsion to touch her. If Maggie were any hotter, she'd be in danger of spontaneously combusting, he thought as he slipped into the cab behind her. But the odd thing was, she didn't flaunt her body in any way. It was as if having dressed, she then forgot about her physical appearance. He just wished *he* could forget about it. But Maggie was starting to shadow his waking thoughts and color his dreams.

Once the cab was in motion, Maggie asked the question that was uppermost in her mind. "Who am I helping you choose a present for?"

"My great-aunt Edwina."

The surge of relief that filled her made her feel momentarily lightheaded. The gift wasn't for another woman; it was for an elderly relative.

"It's her birthday next Saturday and I have no idea what she might like."

"How old is she?" Maggie asked curiously, wondering what it would be like to have relatives. She'd only ever had her mother. Even though her father had been alive up until eighteen months ago, she had never had him. Not in any sense of the word.

"Eighty-one." A fond smile curved his lips. "She's my father's only aunt."

"Is she in poor health?" Maggie tried to think of what to get someone that old. All she could remember was an Ann Landers column she'd read once that said that the elderly didn't appreciate getting more things.

Richard chuckled. "No. She recently took up skydiving."

"Skydiving?!" Maggie repeated incredulously. "That can't be safe."

Richard shrugged. "She says she doesn't have osteoporosis, so she's no more likely to break a bone than someone fifty years younger. She got the idea when President Bush did it for his eightieth birthday. She said if a man could do it, so could she."

Maggie wasn't sure if she should applaud the sentiment or cringe at the possible repercussions.

"She sounds like a bit of a character," she finally said.

"She is *a lot* of a character. What she really wanted to do was go into the family business after she graduated from Vassar, and I think she would have been great at it, but from all accounts, my great-grandfather was a chauvinist of the first water. He wouldn't hear of it. He demanded she marry the son of one of his friends."

"Did she?" Maggie asked.

"No. She went on safari to Africa instead."

Maggie blinked. "I'm not sure I see the connection."

"I think it came under the heading of thumbing her nose at her father's aspirations for her. After Africa, she stopped in Paris until the war broke out. Then she came home for the duration."

"Sounds like she's had a fascinating life." Maggie unconsciously sounded wistful.

"She's certainly had an interesting one," Richard said.

The taxi pulled up on the Avenue of the Americas side of Rockefeller Center and Richard paid the driver while Maggie got out.

"Didn't you want to follow your father into the family business?" she asked curiously once he joined her on the sidewalk.

Richard shot her a quick glance. "Why would you think that?"

Taking her arm, he started to walk down the street.

Maggie tensed slightly as the warmth of his fingers penetrated the thin gabardine of her jacket and zipped along her nerve endings, making her feel restless.

A question. He'd asked her a question. She struggled to focus on his words. It was much safer than focusing on his touch. Or, even more disturbing, on how his touch made her feel.

"I'm not sure. I guess because of your tone of voice when you told me about your great-aunt. Kind of an indulgent exasperation," she finally said.

Richard frowned slightly, caught off guard by her perception.

"My great-aunt is very bright," he finally said. "She was also not financially dependent on her father. Her mother left her a substantial trust fund. But because her father wouldn't let her work in the family business, she's spent her life doing outrageous things. As far as I'm concerned, she's wasted her considerable talents to spend all her time playing."

In her shoes, Richard would have told his father to go to hell and founded his own company, Maggie thought. Richard was the kind of man who didn't let anyone or anything get in his way once he made up his mind to do something.

A shiver chased down her spine. Nor was he the kind of man who would take being jilted well. Although before she faced that hurdle, she had to somehow get him to the point where he was besotted enough to fall in love with her or, at least, with her fashionable persona. The real Maggie Romer, who preferred baggy clothes and quiet evenings at home, would never appeal to him. A totally unexpected feeling of despair engulfed her.

"Hey, there's no reason to look sad," Richard said. "I can guarantee that my great-aunt doesn't care what I think. Believe me, she's every bit as arrogant as her father was reputed to be. You'll see what I mean when you meet her."

Maggie was taken aback by his words. How was she supposed to meet a relative of his who lived in San Francisco? Unless he was planning to invite her to California for a long weekend? A starburst of excitement exploded in her before common sense doused it. He was probably simply making conversation. Something along the lines of that old, male throwaway line "I'll give you a call" when they have no intention of ever coming within hailing distance of you again.

"What about in here?" Richard gestured to the restaurant on the street directly in front of them.

Maggie walked over to read the menu posted on the door. It listed a tempting selection of dishes, and the prices posted were reasonable. For some reason, it was becoming increasingly important to her that they not order anything that she couldn't afford to pay for herself. It might not be entirely rational, but in her mind, it negated the immense disparity between their financial situations. She made a good living, but it was nowhere in Richard's league.

Although if she were to keep one of those quarterly checks . . . The thought tempted her for a moment before she rejected it. Her father might be dead and would never know, but taking any of his grudgingly given money would be tantamount to giving him a victory.

"The grilled swordfish with fruit salsa sounds good to me," Maggie said.

Richard held open the door for her. "Was there anything on that menu for normal people?"

Maggie squinted as she waited for her eyes to adjust to the dim interior. "By that, do you mean high-cholesterol, high-fat and high-calorie?"

"No, I mean high-taste," he said dryly. "I keep reading about the abysmal eating habits of Americans, and yet I swear that every person I've met since I've gotten to New York is a health-food fanatic."

"I am not a fanatic. What I am is a person smart enough to know that you have to eat right to feel right."

"Two, please." Richard addressed the middle-aged hostess who rushed up to them.

"This way." The woman threaded her way through the half-filled restaurant to a booth for two set against the far wall.

Maggie sat on the brown leather seat and accepted the large menu the woman handed them before leaving.

Richard opened his and studied it for a minute. "The chateaubriand sounds good," he said.

Maggie bit her lip to keep from trying to talk him into a fish dish. Why should she care what his eating habits were? She tried to reason with herself. Within a few weeks, he'd be gone and she'd never see him again.

Richard chuckled. "What admirable self-restraint. You're just dying to give me a lecture, aren't you?"

Maggie sighed. "That obvious, huh? Ah, well, you know what they say about converts. They want to change the whole world."

"Allow me to put your mind at rest. I have a cholesterol level in the low eighties. And it has nothing to do with what I eat. I inherited a gene that gobbles up bad cholesterol."

"Are you ready to order yet?" The waitress gave them a bright, professional smile.

"Have you got any ideas yet about what to buy my great-aunt?" Richard asked once the waitress had taken their orders and left.

"Does she have a hobby?"

"Only driving the rest of the family nuts," Richard said.

"Every family should have at least one eccentric," Maggie said.

"Who was the eccentric in your family?" Richard asked, intensely curious about her. Usually, women were only too eager to talk about themselves, but Maggie was reticent to the point of secrecy about her private life.

"There wasn't one. Actually I don't have any living relatives."

She turned with relief when the waitress brought their wine, hoping that it would distract him.

It didn't. "How about when you were growing up?" he persisted. "What were your relatives like?"

"Nonexistent," Maggie said bluntly. "My mother was an only child, and both of her parents died before I was born."

"And your father?" Richard asked and watched as her features took on a frozen cast that could have hidden anything from extreme pain to extreme anger. One thing was clear, though: the very mention of her father raised extremely strong emotions in her.

"They split before I was born. I only saw him once in my life. This is very good wine," Maggie changed the subject, not caring if she had done it awkwardly. She didn't want to talk about either her dysfunctional family or her years in foster care.

There was no reason for Richard to know her background. Even if her plan for revenge worked out, he would still be returning to San Francisco. A sudden sensation of loss engulfed her, making her feel slightly panicky. Her time with Richard was flying.

Richard studied her closed features thoughtfully. So family was a taboo subject. Why? Family was usually one of the first things his dates talked about. Either to brag about their connections or to complain about what a relative had done. But not Maggie. Mentioning family seemed to make her withdraw. Why? For a second, he considered hiring a private detective to check out her background, but he just as quickly discarded the idea. He wanted her to tell him about herself. He wasn't sure why, but it was becoming increasingly important that she trust him enough to confide in him.

"Have you ever thought of living anywhere other than New York?" Richard asked.

Maggie relaxed at the change of subject. "I considered moving into the suburbs because I'd get more space for my rent dollar, but I like the pace of the city, and it's extremely convenient."

"No, I meant leave the whole area?"

Maggie felt a clutch of excitement that she fought to keep out of her voice. Was her plan working? Was Richard starting to think of a future with her?

"Not really," she said.

"One of the major factors in my decision to buy the company was the copyrights it owns on its programs. I intend to expand their use internationally and, since you're familiar with almost all of them, you'd be a natural to train the support programmers."

Maggie glanced down to hide the dismay darkening her eyes. He was talking about a job. Was that why he had been seeing her? So that he could pitch a job to her?

Disappointment seemed to weigh her down. Apparently, despite all the information she'd garnered from her program, she still didn't know enough to appeal to him on a personal level. Or maybe the lack was in herself. Maybe she just didn't have what it took to attract a man of his caliber, no matter what she was wearing.

Although . . . She stared at the salt shaker on the table. He had kissed her, she reminded herself, and that kiss could hardly be classified under the heading of job recruitment. And he had asked her out tonight to help him buy his great-aunt a present. That was hardly job related. Maybe his main interest in her was to recruit her, but it was also possible that he was attracted to her — at least, a little.

Maggie wanted to scream. She felt as if she were floundering around in a fog, unable to see what was perfectly clear to everyone else.

"I'm not irrevocably tied to New York," she finally said. "It's just that I was born and raised here, and I've never had reason to consider leaving."

"Fair enough." Richard decided he'd said enough for now. He'd planted the idea of a move in her mind without actually committing himself to anything. Now he'd leave it to take root.

He felt a flash of excitement at the thought of what fruit his plan might bear.

Chapter Nine

"Now that I've fortified you with a hearty meal, it's time to pay the piper," Richard said.

"Hearty, indeed." Maggie looked down at the chocolate smears on her dessert plate, searching for a crumb she might have missed. Unfortunately, she didn't find one. "That pie was fantastic."

Richard grinned at her blissful expression. "And here I thought you were a health-food fanatic."

"I told you I wasn't fanatical about it. If you eat sensibly most of the time, you can indulge in an occasional dessert with the density of plutonium without worrying about either your arteries or no longer fitting into your clothes."

Richard's eyes skimmed over the way her cotton top hugged her breasts. She didn't need to worry. She looked fantastic.

"Ready?" Maggie stood and smiled down at him, and he felt an odd clutch in his chest as he realized that it wasn't just her sexy body that fascinated him. He liked the person who lived in that body. He liked her upbeat personality and her straightforward what-you-see-is-what-you-get approach to life.

"As ready as I'll ever be. I hate shopping." Richard got to his feet and, placing a hand on the small of her back, guided her out of the restaurant. When Maggie suddenly moved sideways to avoid a waitress with a heavily loaded tray, her blazer rode up and Richard found his hand resting on her bare skin.

A sharp jab of sensation hit him, racing along his nerve endings and collecting in his groin. If he didn't get to make love to her soon, he wasn't going to be fit to be seen in public, he thought grimly. He hadn't gotten this turned on this fast since he'd been an adolescent and his every second thought had been about sex.

Once on the sidewalk outside the restaurant, he took her hand and started walking toward Fifth Avenue.

A feeling of security washed over Maggie as he threaded his hard fingers through hers, a reaction she was at a loss to understand. Life had long ago taught her that security came from within. It didn't come from another person. But even knowing that, she still felt safe around Richard. As if nothing and no one could harm her while she was with him.

Finally deciding that she was simply going to enjoy the evening and not worry about anything, she said, "Have you any ideas at all about what to get your great-aunt?"

"No, that's where you come in."

"You need a personal shopper," Maggie said tartly.

Richard gave her a mischievous grin that tugged at her heart. "I have one — you."

Maggie grinned back, feeling incredibly lighthearted. After they got his great-aunt her present, she was going to invite him back to her apartment for coffee, she decided. And afterwards with a little luck, maybe they could share another one of those incredible kisses. For a moment, an intense longing to involve him in a whole lot more than just a kiss shook her, but she knew she couldn't let him make love to her. Not when their whole relationship was founded on lies. *Her* lies.

No, making love to Richard would be a very bad idea that would haunt her for the rest of her life. She was almost certain it would make other men's lovemaking seem insipid, and she couldn't risk that. Someday, she wanted to marry and have a couple of kids. She wanted to finally belong somewhere emotionally.

For a second, she closed her eyes, trying to visualize the shadowy image of a future husband, but the only face she saw was Richard's, and that was impossible. Everything she'd learned about him highlighted the fact that he wasn't into permanence. And if, for some reason, he ever did start thinking in terms of marriage and children, it wouldn't be with someone like her. A feeling of hopelessness nibbled at the edges of her composure. Wealthy, well-connected men married equally wealthy, well-connected women. It was a fact of life. Women like her and her mother wound up as mistresses. Disposable sex objects.

"Something wrong?" Richard picked up on her sudden depression and she glanced at him uneasily. He was getting much too adept at reading her moods. And that wasn't good. She needed to maintain a bit of mystery to continue to appeal to him. The program had been specific about that.

"Just thinking about what to get your great-aunt," she lied. "You could always go with tradition and buy jewelry."

Richard thought a second and then said, "No, for two reasons. First of all, she views draping oneself in rocks as idiotic and, second, she inherited all my great-great-grandmother's stuff. Nothing I could buy could begin to touch it."

"Your great-great-grandmother was into jewelry?"

"I have no idea, although I suspect it was more a case that her husband bought the stuff to prove that he was better than his brother."

What would it be like to know that much about your ancestors? she wondered enviously. To have such a feeling of continuity?

"Sounds like he had a bad case of sibling rivalry," she said when Richard fell silent.

"Could be. The older brother inherited the family estates in England. All my great-great-grandfather got was a small inheritance from his godfather."

"Which he took to America and made very good?"

"Eventually. First, he went to India and made a fortune there. He also acquired an incredible collection of gemstones."

"That's right," she said slowly. "That exhibit at the Met said that India was a treasure trove of precious jewels. So what made him leave India?"

"The climate got to him. From what he wrote in his diaries, he must have suffered from some rather severe allergies, not that they would have recognized them as such back then. He went back to England, only to find that his brother had gambled away the family fortune and married a middle-class heiress. He disliked her intensely and despised his brother for taking the easy way out, so he went to America."

Of course he would have despised a middle-class heiress, Maggie thought, feeling no satisfaction at having her assumptions verified.

"So how'd he wind up in California?" she asked.

"He heard about the gold rush and decided that there was a lot of money to be made so he bought a sailing ship, loaded it with goods and went west."

"To hunt for gold?"

Richard gave her a quick grin. "Nah, he was a realist. He knew that the better bet would be selling to the miners."

"Did he send back to England for a bride?" she asked.

"No, Boston."

Maggie was so surprised that she stopped on the sidewalk and the lady behind her bumped into her.

"Sorry," she muttered to the annoyed woman. She started walking again and then asked, "How did an unregenerate snob marry a woman from the colonies?"

"Her father owned a huge shipyard and she was his only child, which may have had something to do with it. Although, from all accounts, he was perfectly happy with his choice. Someday, you'll have to read his diaries and you'll see what I mean."

Maggie bit her bottom lip, knowing there would be no opportunity to read his ancestor's diaries. If her plan worked and she got revenge for Sam, Richard certainly wouldn't want anything more to do with her. And even if it did, he would be bound to lose interest in her once a better-looking, more interesting woman showed up. His girlfriends never lasted long.

Don't think about the future, she told herself. *Just treat this evening as a moment out of time.*

"What were your ancestors like?" he asked.

Maggie tensed. What should she tell him? That her paternal grandfather had been a pillar of New York society and that he would have cut her dead if he'd met her in the street? Or maybe that her maternal grandfather had been an alcoholic and a very inept bank robber who'd died in a federal penitentiary. If Richard was one of those people who believed that genetic background was important, he wouldn't even hold her hand for fear of being contaminated.

"They were pretty much average people," she lied.

She looked around, desperate to find something else to talk about, her gaze was caught by a shop behind Richard.

"Look at that," she said. Stopping, she walked over to the window and examined the display.

"Clothes," Richard said. "Old clothes."

"Bite your tongue, you philistine. These are genuine antiques."

"How do you know?"

Maggie chuckled and pointed to the sign in the lower right-hand corner of the window. "The sign says so."

"Actually, I think that ruby dress is a Fortuny," she said. "I saw one at a fashion exhibit at the Smithsonian once, and his style is unforgettable."

Richard searched his memory of all the clothing bills he'd paid up for his various girlfriends for the name Fortuny and drew a blank. Not that it surprised him, the style of the dress on display appeared much too simple to appeal to his girlfriends, although it would look good on Maggie.

His gaze slipped down over her slender figure and returned to the shimmering, silk dress. It fell from the neckline in a cascade of fine pleats. Its classic simplicity would show off her figure to perfection, and its ruby color would enhance the clear glow of her skin and the gleam of her shining hair.

"I've never heard of Fortuny," he said.

"That's not surprising. He was a Spaniard who lived most of his life in Venice. He was immensely popular in the twenties and thirties."

"Do you like it?"

"I love it. But more to the point, I'll bet your great-aunt would like it."

"Edwina?" He took a second look, trying to imagine his aunt's bony figure in it. "You think so?"

"Yes. If it really is a Fortuny, I'll bet it would remind her of her days in Paris because that dress is just the kind of thing a woman with a lot of money and class would have worn."

"Edwina certainly had the money. The class question depends on which of my relatives you happen to be talking to," he said dryly.

"And it wouldn't be your usual run-of-the-mill gift," Maggie insisted. "Come on. Let's go check it out."

Richard went with her, carried along by her enthusiasm. It was that excitement that found an answer in the saleswoman when she realized that they were interested in the dress. She hastily took it out of the window so they could examine it more closely.

"I have the dress's original sales slip," the clerk told Richard. "It's one of two I bought from the estate of an elderly woman who purchased them in Milan in 1932 and then got pregnant and apparently gained a lot of weight during the process. At any rate, she packed the dresses away in her attic where they stayed until her daughter sold everything after her death. The other one is black, and in the same perfect condition."

Maggie reverently touched the shimmering silk. "It's lovely," she said.

"Why don't you try it on, Maggie?" Richard urged. "You're about the same size as Edwina, just a couple of inches taller."

"Yes, why don't you?" the salesclerk seconded. "It comes with a headpiece, which I also have."

"If you try it on, I'll be able to visualize Edwina in it," Richard said, wanting to see Maggie in the dress.

Maggie gave in to the temptation to wear

the beautiful dress, if only briefly, and followed the salesclerk back to the dressing room. She quickly slipped out of her outfit and pulled the dress over her head, sighing in sensual pleasure as it slithered over her body. The silk seemed to sensitize her skin, making her almost unbearably aware of her body. Carefully, she placed the headdress, with its improbable ostrich feather, on her head and faced the mirror. Her eyes widened. She looked . . . different from her normal work day self; she looked exotic, as if she'd wandered out of a thirties spy movie.

"How's it coming?" The salesclerk asked as she pushed aside the curtain. "Oh, very nice," the woman said. "It might have been made for you."

Maggie stepped out of the tiny cubicle.

Richard felt a surge of lust hit him, the intensity of which surprised him. How could something that covered her from collarbone to midcalf be so damned sexy? he wondered incredulously. Maybe it was the fit. He studied the way the soft silk skimmed the feminine curves of her hips before caressing her thighs. And that ridiculous feathered thing she was wearing on her head made her look glamorous, as if she'd been transported here from another time. Transported by the hand of some benevolent god to be his own personal houri.

He swallowed. That dress was made for Maggie, and she was going to have it. Have it and wear it just for him. With nothing on under it. But she wasn't ready to accept an expensive gift from him yet. After they'd been lovers for a few weeks, then he could give it to her. Then she wouldn't have any qualms about accepting a gift from him.

"Very nice," he said, and his voice sounded harsh to his own ears.

"Would you like to see the black dress, too?" the salesclerk asked, encouraged by his expression.

"Show it to me while Maggie changes."

Maggie returned to the change room and hurried back into her own clothes. As far as she was concerned, nothing could compare with the ruby dress, but then an old lady might prefer black. For that matter, ninety percent of New York women seemed to prefer black. Maybe it was just her unsophisticated background showing, but she liked color. Reverently, she stroked the glowing ruby silk, hoping Richard would buy it.

Picking up the dress and headpiece, she emerged from the dressing room to find the salesclerk waiting.

"I'll just wrap these." She smiled warmly at Maggie as she hurried over to the counter.

Maggie joined Richard, who was studying a wicked-looking sword with a thin blade.

"Where's the clerk?" Richard asked.

"She's ringing up the sale before you come to your senses and decide against spending a small fortune on what really is a costume," Maggie said dryly.

"Don't you think I should?" he asked curiously.

"You can afford it."

Richard was taken aback by her prosaic response. Most women danced around the subject of his immense wealth, not that it was ever far from their minds. That was more than clear in the number of hints they dropped about things they wanted. But Maggie seemed to accept his money the same way she accepted the color of his hair. As part of him and not particularly worthy of mention. Nor had she dropped the slightest hint that she wanted him to buy her something. Not only that, but she'd accepted the first date with him when she'd thought he was just a plumber. He hugged the memory to him like a precious gift.

"Yep, I can afford it," he agreed.

"I hope your great-aunt likes it."

She'd like the black one, which was the one he was going to give her, Richard thought. And he had no doubt Maggie would like the ruby dress. Her expression when she'd modeled it for him had been very revealing.

Maggie's voice was subconsciously wistful. "That dress deserves to be worn after having laid in an attic for all those years."

Richard smiled at her and, turning to the salesclerk, accepted the box she handed him.

"There you are, Mr. Worthington. Do stop by again. And if there is anything you would like us to obtain for you, please don't hesitate to call. We can locate almost any antique you want."

"Thanks for your help." Maggie smiled at the friendly woman as she left the shop with Richard.

"That didn't take long," he said. "How about if we take our shopping spoils back to my apartment and have a cup of coffee? We could stop at the video store near me and pick up a movie." He held his breath waiting for her reply.

"Sure," she said.

Richard felt his body first relax, and then tighten in excitement. Just the two of them, alone, together in his apartment. Even though he couldn't make love to her, that still left a lot of possibilities open. Eagerly, he raised his hand to hail a taxi.

He had the cab drop them off at the video store that he'd discovered down the street from his apartment while out walking last night.

"What kind of movie do you feel like?" Richard asked as he looked over the well-stocked shelves.

Maggie read the title on the DVD in front of her, *The Runaway Bride*, and then glanced sideways at Richard's lean body. No bride would run away from him. Not that any woman was likely to get the chance, she thought. Not if the information from her program was accurate.

"Action? Adventure? Romance?" His voice had changed subtly on the last word, but she wasn't sure exactly how. Could he be worried that she might be getting romantic ideas about him? A chill feathered over her skin, raising goosebumps. Could she have somehow telegraphed her growing fascination with him? She couldn't bear for him to think that she was one of those pathetic women who viewed every man they met as a potential husband.

No, she soothed her growing fear. If he worried she was getting ideas about trying to trap him into marriage, he wouldn't have asked her out. The thought steadied her nerves.

"I want to eat popcorn with the movie, so that limits our choice somewhat."

Richard stared at her for a long moment and then finally said, "I'm probably going to be sorry I asked, but what's the connection?"

"Action and adventure films tend to be heavy on blood and gore, and that makes me queasy and queasy precludes eating popcorn."

"You need to develop a stronger stomach to survive in today's entertainment market." He moved farther down the racks. "We could always ask the clerk if there really is a movie called *Attack of the Coed Cannibals*. I've always wanted to see it."

"*Attack of the Coed Cannibals*?" Maggie frowned slightly as she tried to follow her elusive wisp of memory to enlightenment. "That sounds familiar, but . . . Calvin! He and Hobbes were forever trying to rent a movie like that. Did you like that comic strip, too?"

"My favorite. Particularly the series Watterson did on art."

Maggie smiled at him in perfect accord. "My favorite is the strip he did on aliens when Calvin said that the surest sign that intelligent life exists elsewhere in the universe was that they hadn't tried to contact us."

"Personally, I like the ones Watterson did on the environment," said an elderly man who suddenly joined the conversation.

Surprised, Maggie swung around.

"Sorry, didn't mean to startle you," he apologized. "I'm Ralph. I own the shop, and I couldn't help overhearing your conversation. Unfortunately, I think Watterson made the movie titles up because I tried to order them when I first opened up and I couldn't. But if you're looking for offbeat humor, I have one that I bet Calvin would have loved. It's called *Attack of the Killer Tomatoes!*"

He headed down the aisle. Maggie glanced at Richard, who merely shrugged before they both followed the man.

He pulled a DVD off the rack and handed it to her. "There you go. It takes a special sense of humor to really appreciate this one, but I'll bet you two fill the bill."

Maggie accepted the video. "Thank you, I think."

"You'll love it," the man said. "Can I get you anything else? There's a sequel to it," he added helpfully.

"First, I'd better see how I like this one," Maggie said.

She waited while Richard filled out a form, added a bag of microwavable popcorn from the display beside the cash register and paid the fee. When he was finished, he took her arm and escorted her out of the store.

"It really is *Attack of the Killer Tomatoes*!" Maggie studied the DVD as they walked back to his apartment. "I wonder how I missed it?"

Richard passed his card through the electronic lock to get them into the his apartment building and then said, "You were lucky?"

"Or maybe just careless," she said slowly as she read the back blurb. "This sounds like they played it straight."

Richard laughed. "How straight can you play killer tomatoes?"

Maggie felt a warm tenderness unfurl in her chest at his uninhibited good humor. He looked so gorgeous, and he sounded so happy it made her feel happy just to be around him.

Once they were in his apartment, Richard gestured toward the kitchen. "Why don't you go throw our popcorn in the microwave while I put away Aunt Edwina's gift?"

"Okay," she agreed as she made her way in.

Ten minutes later, they were seated on one of the down-stuffed sofas with a bowl of popcorn in Maggie's lap, watching the movie on the big plasma television that had been hidden in a French country armoire.

The film turned out to be hilarious. Maggie couldn't remember the last time she'd laughed so hard.

"Remind me to ask the man for some more recommendations," Maggie chortled when it was over. "That was great."

Richard grinned at her, and she found herself watching the elusive dimple in his left cheek. She couldn't remember when she'd had such an enjoyable evening, and it wasn't as if they were doing anything out of the ordinary. But somehow with Richard, everyday events took on an added sparkle. Just like his eyes. She watched the tiny lights glimmering in his gray eyes.

Her breath suddenly caught in her lungs as she watched them come closer. He took the popcorn bowl that she was clutching like a lifeline out of her hands setting it on the floor, and lightly traced over her lips with his fingertip.

"You have the softest lips," he murmured.

Maggie's eyes dropped to his mouth and a wave of longing washed over her. Her heart seemed to skip a beat and then began to pound with a slow, heavy rhythm. She felt as if time had somehow slowed, wrapping her in an odd languor that made rational thought almost impossible. And yet, oddly enough, her senses felt keener, sharper.

Longingly, she swayed toward him, and it was all the encouragement he needed. His lips swooped, covering hers with a hunger he made no attempt to hide. His tongue darted between her lips, and Maggie jerked in response at the torrent of tingling sensation that poured through her, leaving heat in its wake. Her skin felt supersensitive, almost painfully so.

Blindly, she reached for his head and her fingers slipped through his silky hair, holding him close. Out of nowhere, tremors attacked her body and she strained to get even closer to him. Rational thought was beyond her. All she could do was feel.

Revel in the sensations swamping her. Sensations she had only dimly been aware existed.

Without conscious thought, her fingers fumbled to open his shirt buttons and then slipped inside. She trembled as she felt the crisp hair on his chest scrape across her palm, and she pressed her hand against his skin, trying to absorb his warmth.

Richard jerked when he felt her fingers against his chest. He wanted more.

"Don't rush it." He frantically tried to put the brakes on his reactions, but it was a lost effort. His mind didn't seem to be connected to his body. His hand slipped beneath her top and fierce joy shook him as he felt her tremble when he cupped her breast.

"You're so gorgeous," he murmured against the soft skin of her throat. "It's hard to believe you're real." His tongue darted out to lick at the frantically beating pulse at the base of her neck, and she squirmed in his arms, frantically trying to get closer.

Richard held on to his self-control with monumental effort. He tensed as he suddenly heard a cellphone playing an excerpt from Beethoven's "Ode to Joy."

Maggie was much slower to surface from

the maelstrom of sensuality she was drowning in.

"We could just ignore it," Richard suggested as he nuzzled the skin behind her ear.

Maggie shivered, struggling to figure out what it was they could ignore. When she finally did, a wave of embarrassment flooded her. Richard liked sophisticated women, and she was acting like some sex-starved spinster. All he had to do was touch her and she dissolved into a mindless puddle of need.

Desperately, she tried to gather the tattered remnants of her woman-of-the-world persona around her as she forced herself to move out of his arms. Fumbling for her purse, she groped for her phone.

"I have to answer it. I promised those programmers trying to fix that mess I mentioned earlier that I'd be available if they ran into trouble."

Hoping that he hadn't noticed the way her hands were shaking with suppressed passion, Maggie pulled out her cellphone and flipped it open.

"Yes," she said, hoping she didn't sound as flustered as she felt.

"Maggie, it's me, Emily."

Maggie frowned, wondering why Sam's

former secretary was calling her. They were friendly acquaintances at work, but they had never socialized together. Not only that, Emily sounded frantic, and she was normally unflappable.

"What can I do for you?" Maggie asked.

"I need a favor. Desperately. Maggie, the most awful thing has happened. Sam . . . He had too much to drink and hit a tree. The cops who pulled him out of the car said that there were no skid marks." Emily lowered her voice to a whisper. "It was like he deliberately ran off the road."

"What!" Maggie sat up sharply. She'd never known Sam to drink to excess, and as for what Emily was implying, she didn't believe it.

"He got turned down for a job he'd applied for today and, apparently, it was the last straw. His wife said he came home and started drinking and then he . . ."

Emily paused, took an audible breath and continued, "His wife called me. I'm at their house out on the island with their kids so she can be at the hospital with Sam. I need you to go to the office, access the computers and change the records to show Sam as having picked up the Cobra on their insurance the day he left."

"He didn't?" Maggie repeated in disbelief.

"It wasn't Sam's fault," Emily insisted. "He meant to do it, but he was so distracted by the raw deal he had gotten from Worthington that it just slipped his mind. Please, Maggie, you've got to do this for him. I'd do it myself, but I don't know enough about the programs to backdate something. I can't tell Sam's wife that they don't have insurance! The poor woman has enough to worry about."

"I'll get back to you," Maggie mumbled and then hastily hung up.

"Bad news?" Richard asked.

Maggie turned and looked at him. This whole mess was Richard's fault. If he hadn't fired Sam . . . But why had he done it? The question nagged at her. It hadn't made any sense when he'd done it, and it made even less sense now that she knew Richard. He wasn't being vindictive or unreasonable at work. And yet his treatment of Sam had been both unreasonable and vindictive. And why hadn't Sam's mother-in-law thought to protect Sam's job like she had every other person who worked for the company, right down to the part-time college student who came in afternoons to help file? Unless she had expected Sam and her daughter to live off her? If so, she didn't know her own son-in-law very well.

Sam had far too much pride to become her dependent.

"Yes," she said slowly. "That was Emily Adams, from the office. Sam Moore's in the hospital."

"Oh?" Richard's voice was flat. "Nothing serious I hope."

For a second, Maggie considered telling him just how serious it was, but she decided that the fewer people who knew what Sam had apparently tried to do, the better.

"Car accident," she said, giving him part of the truth. "He got turned down for a job today and was rather distracted."

"I see," Richard said flatly. He looked into her worried eyes and wondered if she was concerned about Moore or herself. Daniel was convinced that Moore had had an accomplice, and Maggie's position as Moore's assistant made her the logical choice. But the better he got to know Maggie, the harder he found it to believe that she was a thief.

Maggie's lips tightened when he didn't add anything.

"I guess I'd better be off. I have a busy day scheduled tomorrow," she said, disappointment at his nonreaction making her sound stilted.

Richard made no attempt to get her to

change her mind. The whole mood of the evening had been ruined by Emily's phone call.

"I'll see you into a taxi," he said as he got to his feet.

Maggie left the apartment with him, suppressing a desire to burst into tears. How could such a perfect evening so suddenly disintegrate into them treating each other like polite strangers.

And she was now faced with a real problem. Retroactively signing Sam up for insurance was definitely immoral, probably illegal and, most emphatically, disloyal to Richard. But she was only involved with Richard in the first place to get revenge for Sam, so why should she worry about being disloyal to him, she wondered in confusion.

She stole a quick glance at him, shivering as she saw his withdrawn expression. No matter what she did about the insurance question, someone was going to be furious with her.

There was no easy answer that would satisfy both sides.

Chapter Ten

The following Monday morning Richard looked up from the contract he was studying as his office door opened to reveal Daniel trailed by the rumpled-looking Jeff Zylinski.

"Jeff has something to report," Daniel said.

Richard felt a momentary clutch of unease at the smug look on Daniel's face. The staff had treated Daniel like a pariah from the minute he'd first set foot in the office two weeks ago and, as a result, Daniel very much wanted to prove that one of them had been conspiring with Moore. And he didn't care which one.

Richard nodded to the chair on the other side of his desk. "Have a seat, Jeff, and tell me what you've turned up so far."

Zylinski lowered his bulk into the leather chair while Daniel hovered in the background like a vulture waiting to feast on the remains, Richard thought acidly before feeling ashamed of his thoughts. He'd told Daniel to find out if anyone else had been part of Moore's scheme. It was hardly fair to get angry because he'd done his job.

"Have you found proof that anyone else was involved with Moore?" Richard said.

"Not exactly," Zylinksi said.

"What do you mean, not exactly?" Richard demanded.

"He means what he's found won't stand up in a court of law," Daniel threw in. "But as far as I'm concerned, it's reason enough to fire her."

"I warned you when you first told me to look into Ms. Romer's finances that you'd have to be careful or you could find yourself in the middle of a nasty lawsuit, as well as an invasion-of-privacy charge," Zylinski said. "And if it comes to that, I won't reveal the source who went through her bank account. He's much too valuable to me to risk the publicity."

Richard felt a prickle of unease slither through him at Zylinski's words. Exactly what had they found out about Maggie?

Daniel snorted. "I'd like to see her try and prove slander. First, she'd have to explain how a woman who makes eighty-five thousand a year can come up with lump sum deposits of just over forty thousand dollars every quarter to her checking account. It has to be her share of the embezzled money. There's no other place it could have come from."

Zylinksi looked pained. "All my contact in the banking industry was able to tell me was that the money was deposited from a numbered Swiss bank account. There's no way to tell whose name is on the Swiss account or who deposited the money into it in the first place. The Swiss take banking privacy laws very seriously. My contact also said that she always withdraws the money in the form a certified check made out to cash the day after it's deposited."

Richard frowned, trying to square what he already knew about Maggie with what Zylinski had found out. He couldn't. If Maggie wanted money badly enough to embezzle it, then why hadn't she made a dead set at him? He'd made his interest in her very clear, and yet she hadn't played on his attraction to get him into bed, where she'd be in a position to wheedle large chunks of cash out of him. Not only that, but common sense would tell her that he'd be highly unlikely to prosecute her if he were sleeping with her.

"Where else could she have gotten the money?" Daniel's strident tones broke into Richard's thoughts. "I looked into her background and she was raised in foster care. You know what kind of people they are."

"No, I don't know," Richard snapped, his intense frustration at the situation spilling out. "How does not having parents who are in a position to care for you automatically make you a suspect for the rest of your life?"

Daniel instinctively took a step backward at the anger in Richard's face.

"I didn't mean . . ." Daniel stumbled to a halt because it was obvious to the other two men that he had meant exactly that.

Poor Maggie, Richard thought. Her childhood must have been hell. No wonder she never talked about it.

"Tell me," Richard turned to Zylinski, "have you one actual shred of proof that Ms. Romer has received stolen money?"

"No, as I explained to Mr. Romanos, it's all circumstantial," Zylinksi said.

"But if it walks like a duck and quacks like a duck . . ." Daniel began and then fell silent at Richard's cold glare.

"I deal in facts, Daniel, not in suppositions. And until you have facts, I'm not interested in your theories," Richard said.

Zylinski stood up, shot Daniel a disgruntled look and then said, "I've taken the investigation as far as I can, Mr. Worthington.

I've traced every transfer of cash that Moore made. I can find no evidence that you could take to the district attorney that anyone in the office was involved with him. I'll have a written report on your desk by the end of the week."

"Richard, you can't just ignore what he's found out about Ms. Romer," Daniel insisted.

"I don't intend to ignore it," Richard said. "Nor do I intend to ignore the fact that you were willing to go off half-cocked on circumstantial evidence or that you authorized trawling through someone's bank account, which is not only a gross invasion of privacy but also damned illegal."

Zylinski coughed. "No one will find out, Mr. Worthington. My contact is very trustworthy. Good day."

Richard nodded.

Once Zylinski had left the room, Daniel burst into speech. "What's wrong with you, Richard? That woman has to be involved up to her neck."

"I said I would look into this myself and I will."

Daniel took one look at Richard's closed face and, with an angry grimace, left.

Richard swung his chair around and stared blankly out the window as he struggled to make sense of what Zylinski had discovered. But no matter what angle he approached the problem from, he couldn't come up with a reasonable explanation for the money in Maggie's account. But neither could he believe she was a thief. There was a crucial piece of the puzzle missing, he finally decided. A piece that would put everything into perspective, and he had to find it.

He had to clear Maggie of Daniel's ugly suspicions. Because he loved her. The totally unexpected bit of self-enlightenment slammed through him with the force of a blow, and he instinctively rejected it.

He didn't love her, he tried to tell himself. He just liked her a lot. Liked her sharp mind and her off-beat sense of humor. And he lusted after her body. But lust was normal. It was healthy. And harmless. Lust couldn't hurt him. Not like love could. Loving someone left you open and vulnerable. Richard winced as he remembered the hell his father had gone through when he'd realized that his only attraction for his second wife had been his money.

An image of Maggie's laughing features formed in his mind and he felt warmth seep through him, relaxing his taut muscles.

Maggie wasn't like his father's second wife, he assured himself. Maggie had been attracted to him when she'd thought he was just the plumber. It was safe to love Maggie. But was there any future in it?

As far as he could tell, Maggie was already committed to her work. She'd given him none of the little hints women usually did to let him know she'd like a permanent relationship. But he didn't know if that was the way she really felt or just a reaction to his rather blunt warning on their first date that he wasn't into marriage.

For the first time, he cursed his habit of being totally up-front about his intentions. This time, it had backfired with a vengeance. But he had four weeks to work on getting her to fall in love with him. The more immediate problem was finding out where that money in her checking account had come from. That had to be cleared up before their relationship could move forward.

Somehow, he had to figure out a way to get Maggie to open up. His gut instinct told him that she hadn't conspired with Moore, but it had been wrong before and there was the troubling question of where those deposits in her bank account had come from.

But how could he broach the subject? He could send for her and . . . And what? he mocked the idea. Say, Oh, by the way, Maggie, while illegally accessing your bank account, I noticed some rather large deposits. Would you please explain them?

He grimaced. Besides, demanding that she explain about the money would automatically put them in adversarial positions, and he didn't want to do that except as an absolute last resort. He needed to find some way to bring the subject up so it didn't sound as if he were accusing her of anything. And it would be easier to do out of the office in a more relaxed setting. He reached for the phone to call her.

"Maggie, you have to do it," Emily insisted. "I told them at the hospital that Sam was covered by our insurance. For God's sake, his wife is already worried out of her mind. We can't tell her that she doesn't have health insurance to pay for the hospitalization and counseling Sam needs."

Agitated, Maggie ran her fingers through her thick curls. "Emily, what you're asking me to do is commit fraud. Sam didn't pay for the Cobra. In fact, he signed a form refusing it."

"That sheet doesn't exist anymore," Emily said in satisfaction. "I retrieved it from personnel this morning before anyone came in. What's the matter with you, Maggie? You were as eager to get revenge for what Worthington did to Sam as I was. Just because the bastard's hot is no reason —"

"Revenge against Worthington is one thing," Maggie broke in. "But what you're asking me to do is alter records for the express purpose of cheating an insurance company."

"And you think the insurance company gives a damn about any of us?" Emily shot back. "They'd as soon cut your throat as help you."

"I am not responsible for their behavior — only my own. And I refuse to commit a felony to help a friend. I'm sorry, but Sam made the choice not to continue his coverage."

"And did he make the choice to be fired? Did he make the choice not to be given a reference?" Emily yelled at her. "What is his wife supposed to do? Sam needs help."

"Think a minute, Emily. Louise is not some penniless victim without any options. She can go to her mother and ask for help. Mrs. Wright not only dotes on her and the kids but also is worth millions. Lots and lots of millions, considering how much she got from the sale of this company."

"And what about Louise's pride? What's she supposed to do with that while she goes begging to her mother?"

"Sometimes pride is too expensive a commodity to hang on to," Maggie said grimly.

Emily stalked across Maggie's tiny office, yanked open the door and then turned and said, "You either change the date on that computer program or, as far as I'm concerned, you're no better than Worthington."

Maggie swallowed against her rising nausea, but she refused to sell out her principles. "I'm not going to do it."

Emily's face twisted with impotent fury. "I don't know why I even bothered to ask. Sam told me you were raised in foster care. Someone with your background wouldn't know the first thing about loyalty." She stormed out, slamming the door behind her.

Maggie gritted her teeth, waiting for the pain of Emily's parting shot to ease. Had her years in foster care really made her incapable of showing empathy? The appalling thought crossed her mind. But it wasn't empathy Emily wanted from her,

Maggie argued with herself. Emily wanted her to sacrifice her self-respect so that Sam wouldn't have to face the consequences of his own stupidity by not extending his insurance coverage.

And it *had* been stupid, Maggie thought. Stupid, shortsighted and self-centered. He clearly hadn't thought about the effect it might have on his family.

But then he hadn't exactly been operating with anywhere near his normal efficiency. She tried to excuse his behavior. Stress did strange things to people, and Sam had certainly been under a lot of it when he'd left. Maybe if she could just make Richard understand. Make him listen. Somehow convince him to give Sam his job back. Or, failing that, to at least give him the reference he deserved. Maybe that would make up for her refusal to alter the insurance records.

She rubbed her forehead, trying to ease the nagging headache behind her eyes. She'd spent an almost sleepless night worrying about what to do, and it was beginning to catch up with her. She wanted the problem of Sam settled, not lurking in the background, tainting her relationship with Richard. She wanted it settled because she loved him.

The appalling thought burst into her mind, driving the color from her face and causing an odd ringing sensation in her ears.

She couldn't be in love with Richard Worthington. She tried to still her rising sense of panic. She didn't know him well enough. But she did, she realized with a sinking feeling in the pit of her stomach. Thanks to her research, she knew him very well, indeed. Although she hadn't really needed all the background information on him, she conceded. All it had taken was one look at his buff body under that sink and she'd gone down for the count.

Damn! Of all the appalling complications . . . She rubbed her temples, trying to ease the tightening band of pain around her head.

Maggie sighed. Somewhere in the universe, the god of irony was probably laughing himself sick. To think that she had set up this whole situation in order to make Richard fall for her. And instead, she was the one trapped in the cage of love. And it *was* a trap, Maggie thought grimly as she remembered the years her mother had wasted as her father's mistress and her excuse that she couldn't help herself, that she loved him.

Her phone rang, cutting into her muddled thoughts, and she reached for it, grateful for the distraction.

"Maggie." Richard's deep voice poured through her, speeding up her heart rate.

"Hi." She struggled to keep her voice normal. It would be humiliating in the extreme if he were to guess her feelings.

"How's your day been?" Richard asked.

Maggie frowned, wondering at the odd note in his voice. He sounded tense, not like his normal, unflappable self. Or was her newly discovered love for him making her supersensitive? Could she be hearing what she feared to hear and not what was really there?

"Fine," Maggie muttered.

"You sound distracted," Richard said.

Maggie briefly considered using his comment as an opening to tackle him about Sam but decided not to. Not over the phone. He could simply cut the conversation short and hang up. In person, he couldn't do that. She needed a neutral location. But where . . .

Richard's chuckle sounded a trifle forced to Maggie's hypersensitive ears. "Make that *very* distracted. Anything I can help you with?"

"No, just design problems." Maggie

struggled to sound normal. She didn't want to put up his guard by letting him know that something was wrong. The odds weren't on her side anyway. According to her program, Richard was not prone to changing his mind, especially not about people.

"You need something to take your mind off work. How about if I get tickets to a show tonight?"

"No, I'm too tired to appreciate it," Maggie said, knowing that she'd have no chance to talk to him in a crowd of people. She needed privacy to make her appeal.

"Why don't you come by my apartment for dinner and we can watch another movie?"

Maggie tried not to dwell on what had happened the last time they'd watched a movie together.

"I'll bring takeout," Richard hastily interjected before she could change her mind. "You won't feel like cooking after the day it sounds like you're having. What would you like?"

"Anything, so long as you include something chocolate for dessert." Maggie breathed a sigh of relief when he immediately fell in with her plans. So far, so good. Now all she had to do was find a way to present Sam's case so that Richard would feel compelled to help.

Despite spending the rest of the afternoon trying to figure out how to make Richard understand about Sam, Maggie still hadn't come up with a viable idea by the time she arrived home.

After showering, she pulled an apricot-colored cotton-and-nylon tank top over her tousled curls, covered it with her white cotton tank top trimmed with crystals and pulled on a tiered silk skirt in graduated shades of orange.

Maggie jammed her feet into a pair of black suede-and-jute wedge sandals and rushed back into the living room to make sure that everything was neat.

She glanced around the room, trying to see it through Richard's eyes. It was not very impressive. Her whole apartment would fit into his living room, with space left over.

Maybe she shouldn't have invited him. She began to second-guess her decision. Maybe being here would make him more conscious of the differences between their social and financial positions.

Uncertainly, she caught her lower lip between her teeth. But where else could she find the privacy she needed? A restaurant was far too public, and she could hardly invite herself to his place.

Maybe there was something in her program that she had originally overlooked that might give her a clue as to the best way to get him to listen about Sam. She glanced at the clock on her wall. She had ten minutes before he was due. That was enough time to ask the program a couple of questions.

Quickly, she turned on the computer and loaded the program.

Maggie stared blankly at the screen as she tried to figure out how to word her question to get an answer she could use. Perhaps . . .

The buzzer from the street-level door broke into her thoughts, and she took a deep breath, willing the sudden attack of butterflies in her stomach to settle. Was that Richard already? He'd always been punctual to the minute. Maybe he was so eager to see her that he couldn't wait a second longer? The idea sent a shaft of excitement through her.

The buzzer sounded again and Maggie hurried over to the intercom beside the door. "Yes?"

"Open the door, Maggie. I'm juggling

sacks and a bottle of wine." Not even the poor quality of the intercom could effectively disguise the sexy quality of Richard's voice. She could pick that sound out of a crowd anywhere, she thought on a rising tide of anticipation.

Hurriedly, she pressed the release for the front door.

"It's open," she said and then counted off the seconds while she waited for him to arrive.

A minute and a half later, there was a muffled thump against her door, and she hastily pulled it open. Happiness flooded over as she stared at him. Rather to her surprise, he looked the same as always. Same ink-black hair that was slightly ruffled, as if the breeze had disheveled it. Same classically carved features. Same sparkling gray eyes that sent shivers down her spine. Somehow, she'd expected him to look different now that she knew that she loved him.

Of course he didn't look any different, she told herself. *She* was the one who'd changed, not him. And if she wasn't careful he might realize it. And if he realized it, he would pity her, and she couldn't bear that. She'd rather he disliked her. Pity was soul-destroying.

"Here, let me take some of that." She grabbed the bottle of wine he had tucked under his arm.

"Where should I set these bags?" He gestured to the two sacks he was carrying.

"On the table." She pointed to her small drop-leaf dinner table, which doubled as an end table.

"I brought Chinese and a chocoholic's sampler," he said.

"What's a chocoholic's sampler?" she asked curiously.

"I haven't a clue. I stopped by the pastry shop for dessert and saw it on the menu." He opened the white paper sack and pulled out a large plastic container filled with five different chocolate concoctions.

"Whoa!" Maggie's eyes widened at the sight. "A cholesterol-watcher's nightmare."

"You don't want it?" Richard asked uncertainly.

Maggie chuckled. "Don't be silly. Have a seat and I'll get us some utensils."

Richard felt his body react as he watched the slight jiggle of her slim hips beneath the thin material of the skirt she was wearing. He clenched his fingers as he fought his compulsion to touch her. To stroke her leg. To caress her thigh and continue upward.

His heart started to beat faster and he hastily put a brake on his thoughts before his reaction became obvious to her. Soon, he comforted himself. Tonight, he'd clear up the matter of that money in her checking account. Then he could take her to bed. But how could he get her to tell him what he needed to know without sounding as if he were accusing her of theft?

He was still racking his brain for a casual opening to the subject when, to his surprise, she did it for him.

"Richard, I need to talk to you about Sam Moore, and I need you to listen to me before you say anything. Promise?"

Richard felt unease slither through him at her tense features. It didn't matter what she told him, he assured himself. He could deal with it.

"I promise," he said.

Maggie took a long breath, trying to marshal her thoughts. "I don't know why you have it in for Sam . . ."

She paused and, when he didn't say anything, continued. "His wife is afraid that the accident he was in on Friday wasn't an accident but a deliberate attempt to kill himself. She said he was very despondent because he was turned down for a job that he was well qualified for. They turned him down because you won't give him a reference."

"Damn right, I won't." Richard's harsh tone was not encouraging, but Maggie forced herself to go on.

"Richard, Sam deserves one. He did a fantastic job for the company for over three years. He increased sales fivefold over what it was when he took over after his father-in-law died. Not letting him remain as president is just plain stupid because you aren't going to stay in New York to run a small company like this."

"True." Richard's calm agreement sent a chill of apprehension through Maggie that had nothing to do with Sam. It was her own bleak future she was seeing. The loneliness she'd have to endure when Richard went back to San Francisco. Determinedly, she shoved her own pain aside to deal with Sam's.

"So who are you going to get that could do even half the job Sam did?"

Could she really not know about the embezzled funds? he wondered. Or did she think he didn't know? Maybe she thought that Moore's mother-in-law had destroyed the evidence before she sold the company. Bookkeeping wasn't Maggie's area of expertise. She might not realize that there would be no way to totally erase an embezzlement of that size. Maybe it was time for him to be blunt, no matter what he'd promised Mrs. Wright.

"I won't keep Moore for the same reason I refuse to be a party to inflicting him on another unsuspecting employer."

Maggie frowned uncomprehendingly. "And what reason is that?"

"In the three years between his father-in-law's stroke and his death, Moore embezzled almost two million dollars," Richard said, closely watching her reaction. Her eyes widened and her face paled, making her skin seem almost translucent. Either she was a superb actress or she really was shocked.

To his surprise, she didn't immediately leap to Moore's defense. Instead, she stared at him for a long moment and then said, "What proof do you have?"

"It came out in the audit when I was negotiating to buy the company."

Maggie frowned, trying to relate what Richard was telling her with what she knew about Sam. She couldn't.

"It doesn't fit," she finally said.

"What doesn't fit?"

"Sam stealing all that money. I mean, if

226

he had taken it, then why would he be desperately looking for another job? And he is. Not only that, but two million is a lot of money to dispose of in just three years. What did he spend it on? I refuse to believe he had an expensive girlfriend tucked away somewhere. Sam was devoted to his wife and his two little girls. For that matter, why take it in the first place? His wife is Mrs. Wright's only child. It's all going to come to her in the end anyway." Maggie shook her head in confusion. "None of it makes any sense."

"It does if you add up the fact that Moore is a compulsive gambler. And you are not to mention that to anyone," Richard warned her.

"Sam?" Maggie repeated incredulously. "That's impossible. Why, he used to make fun of me because I buy a lottery ticket every week. He once told me the odds of my actually winning and, believe me, they were astronomical. So why would he gamble?"

"Why does anyone indulge in self-destructive behavior? Although he didn't buy lottery tickets. From what the detective his mother-in-law hired found out, he was heavily into high-stakes poker."

Maggie shook her head, finding it impossible to visualize Sam as a hardened poker player. Or as a thief.

"Could you be wrong about who took the money?" She gestured impotently. "I mean, could someone have framed him?"

"Who? His mother-in-law? For what reason? She had to eat the losses. You can't write off theft on your taxes unless you are willing to prosecute, and she wasn't about to send her daughter's husband to jail. As for anyone else who might have been helping him, I've had an accounting expert in fraud going through the books with a fine-tooth comb."

Maggie looked up, alerted by something in his voice. His eyes were watchful, and she felt a chill of apprehension slither down her spine. Were the company's books the only thing his expert had gone through? Had he discovered the deposits made to her bank account? But if he had done that, then why hadn't Richard demanded an explanation? Unless he was waiting for her to bring up the subject?

Should she say anything? She tried to think. If he already knew about those deposits and she didn't explain where the money had come from, he might think she'd gotten it from Sam. But if he had any suspicions that she was involved in Sam's embezzlement, then why was he calmly eating dinner with her? He'd kicked Sam out and refused to have anything to do with him. Why would he treat her any differently?

Maggie felt like screaming. She didn't have any answers — just a lot of maybes and she couldn't afford to guess wrong because her whole relationship with Richard could go down the tubes if she did. But it was going to anyway, the unpalatable fact surfaced. In four weeks, he'd go back to San Francisco and she'd be lucky to see him once every five years. The thought made her feel physically sick.

"Are you all right? You look kind of . . . pale."

And so she should, Maggie considered, caught up in a grim mixture of fear at revealing her background and disgust at her own plans for revenge against a man who had done nothing to deserve it.

She took a deep breath, trying to steady her thoughts. She had to tell him the truth about her background. It was the only way.

"I imagine that you came across the deposits to my checking accounts and wondered about them in light of what you've told me about Sam."

Her words caught Richard off guard.

He'd expected to have to lead up to the deposits in her checking account, not have her calmly bring up the subject — although not so calmly. He frowned slightly at how rigidly she was holding herself. She looked tense enough to break, and it was all he could do to resist taking her in his arms. He wanted to comfort her and tell her it didn't matter. That no matter where that money had come from, it would be all right. He'd make sure of it. But he throttled the impulse. First, she had to come clean. They couldn't move forward in their relationship unless there was absolute honesty between them.

"To coin a phrase, it's a long story." Maggie looked down at her hands to find them clenched into fists. With deliberate effort, she relaxed them.

"Go ahead," Richard encouraged her when she fell silent.

"My mother was a very beautiful woman who moved to New York from a small town in southern Indiana. She was not very well educated and naive to the extreme. She met my father and fell in love. He fell in lust and set her up as his mistress. My poor mother was too naive to see that she was just his bit on the side. Anyway, when she got pregnant with me, she apparently expected him to divorce his society wife and marry her."

Maggie sighed and all the hopelessness of her emotionally sterile childhood reverberated in the sound. "She said he laughed in her face and told her to get an abortion."

"Clearly, she didn't." Richard forced a level tone when what he really wanted to do was demand to know who her father was so he could destroy him.

"No, she apparently hoped right up until the day I was born that he'd change his mind. A visit from his lawyer while she was still in the hospital cured her of that fantasy. The lawyer offered her an allowance until I was eighteen, but in exchange, she had to sign a document swearing that she'd never had sex with him. That her claim that he was my father was a lie to try to extort money out of him."

"I take it she signed," Richard said.

"Yeah, that she did. She talked about him incessantly as I was growing up, but she never mentioned his name. I discovered his identity by snooping in her dresser drawer when I was twelve. And I certainly got my just desserts." She swallowed the lump in her throat at the memory of what had happened.

"I went online to find out about him. I discovered that he was a high-powered businessman who came from very old money. I was intensely curious about him, but I didn't try to see him until the following year, when my mother died and they were going to put me in a foster home."

"What happened?"

Maggie shivered. "It was a disaster. He called me a bastard, a mistake that never should have been born. Then he picked up a picture that he had sitting on his desk and shoved it at me."

Maggie wrapped her arms around herself as if to hold in the pain that tore through her at the humiliating memory. "It was a portrait of a girl a couple of years younger than me. She was sitting on a horse, holding a blue ribbon, and my father was standing beside her looking proud. He said *that* was his daughter and as far as he was concerned, his *only* daughter. Then he grabbed my arm, dragged me through the office and literally flung me out into the hallway."

Unable to bear the pain he could see etched in her face, Richard enveloped her in his arms. Cradling her against his chest, he rocked her back and forth, trying to ease the bitter memory.

"Sounds like *he* was the bastard."

"That he was." Maggie gave a watery chuckle. "It kind of makes me afraid of what might be lurking beneath the surface of my gene pool."

Richard dropped a kiss on the top of her head, wishing he'd never forced her to relive the memory.

Maggie took a deep breath, beginning to feel better as the warmth of Richard's body dissolved her icy memories. "Anyway, at some point between then and his death, his lawyer convinced him that if he didn't make any provisions for me in his will, I could contest it as his daughter."

"Would you have?"

Maggie shrugged, and the feel of her body moving against him made his breath catch in his lungs.

"Not this side of hell. I wanted nothing whatsoever to do with that . . ." Her voice trailed off, as she wasn't able to think of a word strong enough to express her contempt.

"I take it he took the lawyer's advice and left you a chunk of money?"

"Not exactly. He left me a trust fund that pays out about forty thousand every quarter. But the trust isn't really mine. I get the income from it during my lifetime, and upon my death, it goes to my kids."

Richard felt relief pour through him, relaxing his tense muscles. She wasn't involved in anything illegal.

"When the money is deposited in my account, I donate it to various charities. He didn't want anything to do with me when he was alive, and I certainly don't want anything to do with his money now that he's dead."

"What about your sister?" Richard asked.

"Half sister," Maggie corrected. "I've never tried to contact her. Somehow she doesn't seem real to me."

Richard's arms tightened around her. He wanted to tell her that her lack of family didn't matter because he was willing to share his with her. But he couldn't. It was too soon. She'd never believe he could have fallen in love with her in the space of two weeks. He'd wait until his six weeks were up and then tell her how he felt and ask her to marry him.

Releasing her, he dropped a quick kiss on the tip of her nose and said, "Why don't you get a couple of wineglasses and —" The ringing phone interrupted him.

Maggie stepped out of the comforting circle of his arms and eyed the phone warily. She had the feeling it was Emily calling to have another try at getting her to falsify the insurance records. She couldn't take the call here. Richard was bound to be suspicious if he heard her half of the conversation. Even if she wasn't willing to do it, she didn't want to get Emily into trouble with Richard.

"I'll answer that in the kitchen while I get the glasses," she said and hurried through the door.

Richard watched the door close behind her and looked around the room. The picture of a much younger Maggie surrounded by three girls which served as a screen saver on her big computer drew him like a magnet and he walked over to take a closer look.

It was very impressive. Just what he would have expected a computer expert to have. Realizing the machine was on, he touched a key to see what she'd been working on. He was insatiably curious about everything to do with her.

The screensaver dissolved and Richard frowned as he saw his name in the document she had open.

Curious, he leaned closer. An icy feeling lanced through his stomach and spread outward, numbing him as he realized he was looking at a list of the women he'd dated over the past five years, along with their individual characteristics.

The numbness began to dissipate, blown away by the anger that exploded inside him. Quickly, he backtracked to check the date the program had been created. Three weeks before he'd arrived in New York. He didn't know what this program was or what it did, but one thing was clear: Maggie had known all about him before she'd ever laid eyes on him. She must have come to the apartment expressly to meet him.

Rage and hurt ripped through him, making it difficult for him to breathe. To think that he'd actually been stupid enough to believe that she'd been attracted to him, not his money. And all that time, she'd been setting him up.

It was his father's second marriage all over again. Hell, Maggie made his father's grasping second wife look like a rank amateur.

"Richard, I . . ." Maggie came to a halt as she realized with horror that she'd forgotten to turn the computer off. And Richard was looking at it.

"Don't say anything!" he gritted out. "I've never hit a woman in my life, but at the moment, the urge is almost irresistible."

Maggie pressed her lips together to stop them from trembling as she tried to figure out what to say and how to make him understand, but fear had blanked out her mind.

"Don't come back to the office," he bit out. "Your personal effects will be mailed to you."

"But . . ." Maggie raised her hand in a mute plea for understanding, but he brushed past her. With a feeling that her whole world was collapsing, she watched him walk out the door.

Chapter Eleven

Richard stared blankly at the proposal on the desk in front of him, realizing that he couldn't remember a single solitary fact from it. Not even the name of the company involved.

"Hell!" He dropped his head into his hands. He couldn't sleep, he couldn't eat, and now he couldn't work.

He rubbed his bloodshot eyes and tried to focus again on the proposal. It was impossible. All he could see was Maggie's face as he'd last seen it four days ago in her apartment. She'd looked shattered when he threw her out of his life. But the question was, had she been shattered because one of the richest men to ever cross her path had seen through her schemes or because . . .

Don't go there, he tried to tell himself. She can't love you. You saw that program. It was a setup from start to finish. Face it. You were had by an expert.

"Damn!" He shot to his feet, too upset to sit still. He'd told himself that the pain of her betrayal would fade. But it hadn't. In fact, it hurt more now than it had four days ago. He missed her. He missed everything about her, from her sharp mind to her sexy body. His desire for her had grown to an all-encompassing craving that seemed boundless, and he didn't know what to do about it.

Maybe if he cut his stay in New York short and returned to San Francisco . . . He shuddered at the thought of leaving. Of putting three thousand miles between them. Of never seeing her again.

Agitatedly, he shoved his fingers through his hair. His indecisiveness made him furious. He wasn't an indecisive man, but without Maggie, he'd become one. Without Maggie, he seemed to have lost his way. Grimly, he stalked over to his office window and stared down through the darkness at the headlights of the cars illuminating the city streets far below.

"Think, Worthington," he ordered himself. "You can't go on this way. Somehow, you have to get over her."

The sound of the actual words vibrating in the air made him realize just how hopeless the idea was. He wasn't going to get over his love for Maggie like it was some kind of twenty-four-hour bug. He loved her, dammit! He'd waited thirty-two years to fall in love, and once he'd done it, he'd put his whole heart and soul into it. There wasn't going to be an easy way to forget her. Somehow, she'd entwined herself around his heart, and his attempt to cut her out was leaving him raw and bleeding.

Okay, if his chances of forgetting her were nil, then what were his options? He tried to think logically. The only alternative he could come up with would be to marry her anyway. To bind her to him so tightly that she'd eventually forget why she married him.

Maybe his love would spark a similar response in her in time. Who was it who'd said that marriage was what you made of it? He didn't remember; he just prayed the guy was right. Richard took a deep breath and slowly expelled it, feeling an odd peace steal over him.

He frowned as he suddenly remembered what she'd said the last night they were together. For the first time since he'd seen that program, he listened to his head and not his lacerated pride and turbulent emotions.

If money was that important to her, then why had she given the proceeds of her trust fund to charity? She was getting forty thousand a quarter. That was a hundred and sixty thousand a year. Why hadn't she spent it on herself or even saved it to spend later? Even more telling was the fact that she'd been giving the money away since before he'd bought the company, so she couldn't have done it to impress him. But if she didn't care about money, then why had she written a program whose clear intent was to trap him? She couldn't have loved him because she'd never even met him, so what had her motive been? Why hadn't she been actively hostile to him like everyone else in the office had been?

Richard rubbed the back of his neck. He didn't have a clue, and the only one who could tell him was Maggie, provided she was even willing to talk to him after the way he'd forcibly kicked her out of his life.

He checked his watch. It was only ten. She wouldn't be in bed yet and, even if she was, she'd wake up soon enough when he told her he was willing to marry her. Although . . . A frisson of fear slithered down his spine. The nagging feeling that he was missing something, something vital, refused to go away as he headed toward the door, intent on having this out with her tonight.

Determined not to lose her nerve and run away, Maggie took a deep breath and reached for the doorknob. This was definitely one of those instances where surprise was of the essence — at least, she hoped it was. Her hand had almost touched the knob when the door suddenly opened and she found herself staring into Richard's lean features.

She wondered if the shock on his face was mirrored in her own. Her eyes slipped over his face, noting the lines of tiredness carved beside his mouth. He looked as miserable as she felt, a spark of hope burst into life. He might have thrown her out of his life, but he didn't look too happy about it.

"I have to talk to you," she rushed into speech before he could say anything. Since Richard had stormed out of her apartment four days ago, she hadn't slept more than a few hours at a time, and the very thought of food made her feel nauseous. She wanted Richard with an intensity that seemed both boundless and hopeless. One thing that accursed program had shown her was that he was not a forgiving man. Fortunately, Richard hadn't thought to tell the guard that she was not to be admitted after hours.

Richard squashed the intense relief he felt at simply being near her. First, he'd listen to what she had to say and then he'd tell her he was willing to marry her, but on his terms. And then he'd take her home and make love to her until she couldn't remember why she'd wanted to marry him in the first place.

His eyes narrowed slightly as he studied her. And after that, he'd feed her. She looked like she'd lost weight, and she didn't have any to spare.

Stepping back, he retreated into his office. He sat down on the corner of his desk and gestured her into the chair, wanting to get the words out of the way so he could take her in his arms.

Maggie sat down, oddly glad of the space between them. It provided a barrier to the lure of his body, which was making it hard for her to concentrate on what needed to be said.

"So tell me about the program," he clipped out.

Maggie winced at his sharp tone. "I wrote that program before I ever met you."

"To marry my money," he said flatly.

Maggie looked up, jarred out of her jumbled thoughts by his erroneous assumption. "No! I don't need your money. I earn a good salary. Plus, if money were that important to me, I would use what my father left me instead of giving it away."

Richard felt his tension ease slightly at her emphatic tone. Simple logic told him she was telling the truth — about the money, at least.

"Then why did you write it?"

Maggie caught her lip between her teeth as a flush washed over her pale skin. She felt deeply ashamed of her motivation in light of what she now knew. But Richard deserved the truth — all of it.

"I wrote it for revenge. I wanted to pay you back for what you had done to Sam. My goal was to make you fall in love with me and then to —" she gulped "— walk out on you."

"I see," Richard said slowly, feeling warmth spark to life deep inside him. Her misguided desire for revenge, he could understand — and forgive because it hadn't been directed against him personally. She'd wanted revenge on a stranger by the name of John Richard Worthington, whom she thought had injured a good friend of hers.

"I doubt it," Maggie muttered, "because I'm not sure that I see what happened after that. I don't know if it was because I knew so much about you to start with or if it was just being around you but . . ."

Maggie hesitated, torn between not wanting to tell him she was in love with him and exposing herself to more rejection and knowing she owed him the truth.

"I fell in love with you," she finally blurted out.

Richard felt a euphoric sense of release rush through him. It was all he could do not to reach down and grab her. But it was too soon for that. First, they had to clear this up. Clear it all up.

"And what about Sam?" he demanded.

Maggie shook her head. "You were justified in firing him, and I guess you couldn't give a man who embezzled millions a reference, but I still think he needs help, and he has a lot to contribute once he conquers his addiction."

"Maybe," he muttered, "but to be frank I don't give a damn about Moore at the moment. Come here," he ordered.

Maggie got to her feet and moved toward him on legs that felt wobbly. She loved him so much, and it was hard to tell what he thought from his closed expression.

His hand suddenly reached out and he grabbed her wrist. Maggie let out a surprised squeak as he pulled her between his hard thighs. His arms closed around her and he held her so tightly against his chest that it was a challenge to breathe.

"I missed you so much." He buried his face in her hair, breathing in the light floral scent that clung to her.

"Oh, Richard!" Maggie burst into tears.

Richard held her away from him and stared worriedly into her face. "Why are you crying?"

"Relief, I think. I've been so miserable."

"You aren't the only one. I couldn't believe how much I missed you. Why don't we go back to my apartment and get a flight first thing in the morning?"

"To where?" she asked absently, her whole concentration on the thought of going back to his apartment with him.

"Vegas. We can be married ten minutes after we step off the plane."

"Married!" Maggie stared up into his beloved face. "But you can't marry me."

"Why not?"

"Because if you do, you'll always wonder why I married you."

"I know why you're going to marry me. You told me. You love me. And since I love you to distraction, I intend to marry you quickly before you change your mind, which means Vegas. Unless you've got your heart set on a long, white dress, a thousand guests and two thousand headaches." He winced at the thought of having to wait months to put a ring on her finger.

"You love me?" Maggie repeated.

"Totally, absolutely, irrevocably," he said. "And in my book, that means marriage. The only point up for negotiation is when and how."

"Actually, I always wanted to be married by Elvis. But you don't have to marry me."

"And how would we explain that to the kids?"

"What kids?" Maggie asked in confusion.

"I told you the first time I met you, I was going to have a family."

Maggie considered the idea for a second and found it incredibly seductive. To actually belong to a family. To be part of a close-knit group who loved one another.

"I like the idea of kids, but I'm still worried that you might someday think . . . I know," she said excitedly, "I can sign a prenup saying I relinquish all claims to your money."

"Forget the prenup. Forget everything but that we love each other," Richard said a second before his lips closed over hers. Maggie relaxed against him, finding his order surprisingly easy to follow.

Epilogue

"Mom, mom!" Jack rushed through the French doors onto the patio. "My stock just split. I told you that company was going to be a winner."

Maggie brushed his silky black hair back from his forehead and smiled into her eight-year-old son's excited face.

"That you did, kiddo. Keep going like this and you'll be able to support me in my old age."

"Grandpa says I'm a natural," Jack said proudly.

"A natural pain in the —"

"Simon," Maggie eyed her six-year-old warningly.

Simon gave her an angelic grin and said, "I was going to say neck, Mom. Give me the pliers, Philip."

"Please," Maggie inserted.

"I'll bet doctors don't say 'please' in the operating room when they ask for an instrument," Simon complained.

"They do if they have good manners, and you aren't operating. You're building a crystal radio set."

"Can't find 'em," his three-year-old brother announced.

"They have to be here," Simon said. "I just used them to . . ." He paused and turned to look at a huge, gray furry shape sleeping on one of the loungers.

"Zeke, did you take the pliers."

Zeke lifted his head, gave the boys a doggy grin and ambled into the house.

"Quick, let's follow him," Simon ordered his brother. "Maybe he'll lead us to them."

The two boys tore off after the dog.

"I'm going to go call Grandpa and tell him about my stock," Jack said.

Maggie leaned back in the lounger and let her breath out on a long sigh, feeling so happy she could hardly contain it.

"What does that sigh mean?" Richard's deep voice sent a shiver of awareness through her and she started to struggle to her feet.

"Don't get up." He leaned over and placed a warm kiss on her lips that sent a shaft of desire zinging through her.

"You're early," she said, pleasure lighting up her face.

"I got to thinking about you and suddenly work didn't seem all that interesting. How are you and Eleanor and Eugenia doing?" He gently patted the huge mound that was her abdomen.

"Hanging in there — just."

"Only four more weeks," Richard comforted her. "I never thought that when we tried one more time for a girl we'd wind up hitting the jackpot."

"I hit the jackpot when I met you. The kids are simply a bonus. How was your day?"

"Busy. I got a call from Sam Moore. He and Louise and their daughters will be here in San Francisco next weekend. Their oldest is considering attending Stanford and they want to check it out. I invited them over for dinner. Louise is going to call you to set up a time."

"It'll be good to see them again."

"Hmm," Richard murmured. "Sam wants to talk to you about that inventory control program you wrote for that Greek shipping firm. He said he's had feelers from a firm in Hong Kong, but they need some specialized refinements."

"Did he say what kind?"

"No, but I have no doubt he'll sell it to them. You were right about the guy. He could sell snow to Eskimos."

Maggie caught his hand and placed a kiss on his palm. Sometimes she loved him so much it hurt. "And he has you to thank for giving him a second chance."

"No, he has you to thank. I did it for you. Once he beat the gambling, he's been an exemplary employee. I . . ."

Richard broke off as the dog came tearing through the French doors, a pair of silver pliers hanging from his mouth. A second later, he was followed by Simon and Philip who stopped when they noticed their father.

"Dad." Philip wrapped his arms around his father's legs and Richard picked him up.

"Hey, sport, what's going on?"

"Zeke's being a dog. Will you help us get our pliers back?" Simon demanded.

"Sure. Be back in a minute, love. Don't move." Richard threw a kiss at Maggie, who watched him go, her heart in her eyes.

The employees of Thorndike Press hope you have enjoyed this Large Print book. All our Thorndike and Wheeler Large Print titles are designed for easy reading, and all our books are made to last. Other Thorndike Press Large Print books are available at your library, through selected bookstores, or directly from us.

For information about titles, please call:

(800) 223-1244

or visit our Web site at:

www.gale.com/thorndike
www.gale.com/wheeler

To share your comments, please write:

Publisher
Thorndike Press
295 Kennedy Memorial Drive
Waterville, ME   04901